PENGU

A L
IN THE BLACK

The town was already dying the day the stranger arrived on the train. Jules saw him first – a shadow in fading light, far across the waste ground. From that moment on, everything began to change: not only for Jules but for everyone else around.

Now the town's future hangs in the balance. Every day brings a new dark miracle. For the intruder knows everyone's innermost desires and dreams. He knows all there is to know about everyone. He can do anything anyone wants . . . *anything* at all.

He could be a saviour . . . so why is Jules terrified by his presence? What is the purpose behind his power? And why did he really come here?

A gripping and frightening fantasy from a talented new author, *A Light in the Black* was short-listed for the Guardian Children's Fiction Award.

Chris Westwood was for three years a journalist on the music weekly, *Record Mirror*, before studying film and TV production at Bournemouth. He is now a full-time writer, writing novels for adults as well as teenagers, and lives near Pontefract, West Yorkshire.

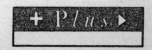

By the same author

Calling All Monsters
Personal Effects

CHRIS WESTWOOD

A LIGHT
IN THE BLACK

PENGUIN BOOKS

PENGUIN BOOKS

Published by the Penguin Group
Penguin Books Ltd, 27 Wrights Lane, London W8 5TZ, England
Penguin Books USA Inc., 375 Hudson Street, New York, New York 10014, USA
Penguin Books Australia Ltd, Ringwood, Victoria, Australia
Penguin Books Canada Ltd, 10 Alcorn Avenue, Toronto, Ontario, Canada M4V 3B2
Penguin Books (NZ) Ltd, 182–190 Wairau Road, Auckland 10, New Zealand

Penguin Books Ltd, Registered Offices: Harmondsworth, Middlesex, England

First published by Viking Kestrel 1989
Published by Penguin Books 1991
3 5 7 9 10 8 6 4 2

Lyrics on page 165, from the song 'Be Brave' from the LP 'Sleep No More'
Copyright © Comsat Angels, 1981, used by permission of Desert Songs
under licence to S.B.K. Songs Ltd, 3–5 Rathbone Place, London W1P 4DA

Printed in England by Clays Ltd, St Ives plc

To my mother and father —
with love

- PART ONE -

Dog Toys

1

He came to the town in the early summer, only two clear months after they closed the mine. He came in kneeless jeans and sneakers without laces, a skip to his step, his big harmless eyes upturned to the sky, his mouth smiling darkly. He came without fuss and he came unannounced – there were no brass bandsmen at the station, on the platform, to meet him; no flags and banners flying between shops in the streets. He came to the town, this dull little charcoal-looking town, because someone had called him.

And he always heard the calls.

Sometimes he heard them in the quiet of the nights. He heard them as he walked in this or that forest, places where even the moon-time creatures huddled and hushed where he passed. He heard the voices as he journeyed between towns, following canals and motorways and cart-tracks, ditching the contents of his knapsack here and there, in this town or that one. The voices sailed in on the breeze, whispering soft as night air; and sometimes, when they all came at once, all pleading, all whining, all wanting, he cracked his knuckles and sighed, 'I'll give you what you want; I'll give you *all* you want, and more besides!'

So now he stood on the station platform, feeling the summery breeze on his face, hearing only the train, far-gone, far-off, more distant. He opened his lungs to breathe in the town, to taste its air.

Coal fires. Roses.

More coal fires than roses.

Diesel oil, fresh-mown grass, perfume.

He stopped and looked around. The perfume wafted down-wind from a girl standing fifteen, twenty yards along the platform. If she smelled like that in the open air, how did she smell indoors?

Lifting his knapsack, he sniffed and started off along the platform to the steps at the end. The steps climbed upwards to a road bridge and the town and the smell of coal fires, but before he could reach them the girl stopped him with a look. Her eyes were nervous little hamster eyes, looking ready to scamper away rather than stay here and watch him, but she asked him suddenly, 'Where are you from?'

'From out of town,' he said.

The girl frowned, puzzled. 'From that train?'

He looked along the track and back. 'Sure. Why not?'

'How did you get off?'

He shrugged. How many ways could you jump off a train?

'That train', the girl said, 'never stops here. It always goes through like it did just now. *Whoosh!* Fast. So how'd you get off?'

He shrugged again, then smiled his darkest smile. 'I jumped.'

'I don't believe you. I never saw you.'

'Do you only believe the things you can see?' he asked. Somewhere in the distance, another train sounded, approaching, and at once the girl looked ready to run from him.

'I don't believe you could jump off a speeding train and not cripple yourself or something,' the girl was saying. 'Bet you just walked along the track and you're having me on.' She lowered her gaze, began to study her shoes. 'What do you want to come to a town like this for anyway? It's dead as a dodo, mister. You won't find anything here.'

He didn't reply, but looked back along the platform to the incoming train, a local one. It came in slowly, brakes wheezing. The girl began moving towards it, not looking back, and as she did so he began to know all about her – the job she'd lost at the factory, her family . . . yes, her family. That's why she appeared so tense and uptight. As the train pulled in and the doors began opening, he called, 'You don't need to fret, you know! Your mother's fine!'

The doors were still open, yet the girl hadn't boarded. She'd stopped as if stung. She turned back to look at him, eyes wide, jaw dropping.

He smiled his dark smile, then added, 'Sure she's fine! I know all about what happened; but listen, she'll be out of intensive care before you know it!'

The girl stood motionless. 'How did you know she was in –'

'But that's where you're headed, isn't it? The hospital? Don't miss your train,' he added finally.

Doors were slamming behind the girl. A British Rail guard worked methodically along the platform, checking, slamming. For what seemed a whole minute the girl stood ashen-faced, watching the man in his scruffy kneeless jeans and laceless sneakers, the big dark grin all across his face. Then she called, 'Mister, you're not for real! Who the hell are you, anyway?'

But he skip-walked away, hoisting his knapsack more comfortably about his shoulder, sniffing the air, grinning.

Sure as a dog barks, he knew all about her, and her family, and how long her mother had until she came out of intensive care. He knew a lot of things. He knew about people, for instance. He knew how this town had seen the closure of its mine, throwing twelve hundred men in the dole-hole; and he knew how many families wanted to leave and find work elsewhere and couldn't afford to. He knew how the kids were bored, and how some were angry, and how some went ripping up fences by night while others went joyriding.

He walked up the steps to the road bridge and the town and the smell of coal fires, knowing at once there was much to be done here. He walked with a skip and a smile, knowing there was no rail-ticket in his pocket – who needed a ticket when you could make the station-master fall sound asleep over his tea-mug, just by putting your mind to it? So the station-master was softly snoring, and the town seemed half-asleep too, not expecting him; and someone, somewhere in town was calling him.

He knew the girl would never have believed him if he'd told her the truth about the train. That was something else he knew; how he'd sat in first-class and imagined himself out of the train and on the platform;

how just imagining himself there was enough to do the trick. He knew she would've scoffed at that, only believing the things she could see, but that was the plain God's honest truth. But no one else would believe it either; no one else would believe the things he could do, not until they saw *all* he could do.

At the top of the steps he came to the rail station sign, moving his lips as he read the name: EASTFIELD. Traffic on the road bridge passed him by without a second glance, and up here he could smell so much more clearly the smells of the town, the dirt, the grime, the smells of a town on its dying legs. He could almost hear silence in the air – a silence once filled with the chug of mineworkings. Now there was only the purr of factories, the chirrup of schoolkids fleeing schools.

Yes, he could do something here, with this charcoal town. That was another thing he knew. He could raise up the town or destroy it. He could do as he pleased. Wasn't life grand?

Below him, the girl's train yawned into motion, began creeping from the station. He watched for a while from his place on the bridge, just until the train began to look small and bug-like in the distance. Then he turned down towards town; he started to walk.

2

After school, Jules gathered together his odds and sods, his textbooks and files, and walked home. Home was one of the new housing estates on the fringe of town, and to get there you had to trudge up and across a full square half-mile of waste ground. Six months ago, they'd started demolishing the old redbrick terraces that stretched all the way between West End Lane high school and home, and now there was nothing but rubble – bricks, dust, broken stones. No one knew what the council intended to do with the land now it was cleared and flattened; perhaps they'd leave it the way it was.

To Jules the waste ground looked like a photograph torn from a history book: a faded black and white of one of those blitzed war-time English cities, except that here the damage had been done by bulldozers, not bombs. A scattering of bricks marked the spot where a chip shop had stood on the corner of York Street, a shop whose windows had glowed like beacons at night, its doorway buzzing with customers, moths round a flame. Now it was dust.

And the scavengers had had a field day, judging by how little lead and good wood and glass they'd left.

Some had been out with their wheelbarr
out wiring for copper, splitting up doors
for firewood, using the rest of the gear
their walls and windows at home. Ther
here – blank-eyed Easter-leavers, most of them – who
seemed to have nothing better to do than spend their
spare time trashing windows and fences. At night
they'd devote hours to standing in groups on dim-lit
street corners, doing nothing at all, not even talking;
and there were those who'd start an enchanted evening
playing soccer with Coke cans, and end it by either
beating hell out of one another or some pin-striped
businessman's garden wall. And in Eastfield, if you
didn't repair what was broken no one else would.
Some people broke things, others paid the price: that
was the way it went. Shop windows on the high street
were whitewashed, as if awaiting a holocaust; others
were boarded up, decorated with graffiti. Piece by
piece they were tearing the town apart, what was left
of it; and, where the kids weren't demolishing property,
the council was.

Jules had gone as far as Faith Street, or what used
to be Faith Street, when he first caught sight of the
figure. It must have been the figure of a man, loitering
near a still-standing lamppost, but from here and in
the fading light it was hard to tell; the figure looked
nothing more than a blurred grey shape. Yet how
many blurred grey shapes beckoned and smiled, as this
one did?

Jules faltered forward, suddenly cold. A wind was
beginning to stir across the open expanse of waste
ground, and the warmth, for the minute at least,

...ed drained from the day. Overhead, clouds gathered, spoiling the summer sky. Ash-grey dust rose from the ground like a veil, forcing Jules to squint through three-quarter closed lids. The man, if it was a man, was probably just another scavenger, here to comb the rubble in broad daylight for trophies. Somewhere nearby metal rushed over metal – the sound of a train, either nearing town or departing it. Why did the figure seem less like a man and more like a shadow as Jules stepped closer? For a moment he thought he could see the shape raise its arms, its smile fade, its body become still and attentive as if listening for something. Surely no shape, no shadow did that.

Then the sound of the train was thickening in his ears, changing, becoming the beat of his heart and the drag of his lungs. The school was now impossibly far behind him on West End Lane, its Lego-block buildings turning grey under a darkening sky. Traffic moved past in an endless stream. He shouldn't head back – no, that would be senseless; he'd be running from nothing, from a shadow couched under a lamppost. As he reached the junction – what once was the junction – of Faith Street and Cambridge Street, clouds scattered overhead, a hazy sun beamed, and the figure vanished before him like dust on the wind.

Strange, but for a minute, Jules thought, *for a minute there I could've sworn* . . .

It was his vision playing tricks, or his nerves perhaps. That was why, briefly, the shadow had appeared like a man. In a town like this, at a time like this, anyone's nerves might snap at a stroke, or their eyes see visions. He wasn't the only one wishing for something to happen, something out of the ordinary; he couldn't be stuck here forever, please God! In a matter of weeks there'd be exams to face, and after exams the YTS, and after that - he stopped. There was really no sense in worrying that far. You could only hope; you could only wish.

Before he knew it, the light had returned, the sky had blued, and he'd reached Mount Temple with its flat-roofed little box-houses and bungalows in neat little rows, all partitioned in neat little streets. To Jules they looked like Cornflakes packets stuffed together on supermarket shelves. Boxes, boxes, and more boxes. *You live in a box all your life*, he thought, *and in the end they bury you in one just the same*. Here was Mount Temple Drive, Mount Temple Grove, Mount Temple Walk . . . and then, the screaming blunder of all time, Mount Temple Mount, which at least proved the town planners had a sense of humour – either that or they were completely insane.

When he turned in at Mount Temple Crescent, he found Laurie outside, running barefoot down to the sandpit at the bottom of the back lawn. Toby, her little dog, waited patiently in the sand, not even flinching when she tripped and landed beside him.

'Toby hurt his paw,' Laurie said when Jules came in, closing the gate behind him. 'He cut it on some glass.'

'He isn't complaining now,' Jules said.

'He did, though, before. He's been whining all afternoon. It hurts him. I *know* it does.'

Jules was briefly tempted to ask for a sight of the blood, but said nothing, instead trooping up to the house. Toby could stand it all right; he'd had enough bumps and scrapes to be practically immune by now, and once had been squashed beneath the wheels of their father's car on the drive without even a bruise to show for it. Toby had been in good shape for fifteen years, since Jules's first birthday, and would probably be in good shape for fifteen more. Give him a new set of eyes, give his wheels a fresh lick of paint, and he'd look good as new. Laurie had only just turned six, and six wasn't much of an age at all, but how long before she worked out that the damn hound was only a toy, that he felt nothing, whatever you did to him?

'I *know* he's a toy,' Laurie was wailing after him. 'But it still hurts him! Look! Don't you even want to see where he's cut?'

Jules went into the kitchen and set down his books, then pulled up a chair and a pack of digestives at the kitchen table. From here, if he craned his neck just slightly, he could see his sister at the foot of the garden, petting her toy dog on wheels, explaining to him how she'd bandage the paw when mother came home.

He munched a biscuit, not really tasting it, wishing he hadn't agreed to meet Dave Brookman tonight. Nine o'clock: Good God. There was no telling where a night out with Brookman might lead. If he'd really put his mind to it, he might instead have been out with the girl of his dreams, the girl he'd seen for the first time today. He'd been sitting with Steve Harper in the fifth form common room when he first caught sight of her – a new girl, pretty as you please, chestnut-eyed and chestnut-haired, with a shy kind of smile on her face when she looked at him.

'What're you waiting for?' Steve Harper had hissed behind his maths book, holding the book like a mask. 'She just *smiled* at you, didn't she? What're you waiting for?'

Jules had been waiting for the fear to leave him. But it was always like that – easy enough to talk with the girls you didn't like, scary as a walk through the valley of the shadow of death with the ones you did. Instead of smiling right back at her, he'd crumbled, embarrassed. Blown it completely. Then later, he'd asked around and found that her name was Rachel – no one seemed to know much more about her than that, where she was from, what she was doing in a dud town like Eastfield. But Rachel was enough to be going on with; Rachel who'd smiled at him, Rachel who he wouldn't be seeing tonight because he'd sworn to meet Brookman. What a screw-up.

He was into his second biscuit when Laurie came in the kitchen, her bare feet trailing in sand.

'That man came round before you got home,' she said, joining him at the table.

'What man?' Surely she couldn't mean Brookman; he shuddered to think of the language Brookman could teach her if he found her alone. 'Did he come to see me?'

'No, he came to see me,' Laurie said. 'I saw him outside the school today and he waved at me.'

'Someone you don't know?'

'I suppose so.'

'And then he came here?'

Laurie nodded. 'I told you that part already. I –'

'Christ, Laurie,' Jules jumped in. 'How many times

do you have to be told? You've heard all the lectures before.'

'This was different,' Laurie said. 'He was a nice man.'

'I'll bet. *Would you like a sweetie, little girl?* I'll bet he was nice,' Jules said. Easing himself up from the table, he went to the sink, began filling the kettle. 'What did he want?'

'He didn't want anything. Anyway, I wasn't all alone with him if that's what you think. Grandma was in.'

Jules gave a shrug. 'So what's new?'

Grandma was always in. She'd been with the family almost four years, ever since her husband died – a lifetime's mining and smoking had finally killed his lungs, and him with them. Now she spent most of her hours in bed. Much of the time she slept. The rest she spent reading, or recounting her better years to anyone who'd listen. With Grandma upstairs, the house so often felt empty, and on quiet afternoons you'd hear a groan and a footstep up there and jump through your skin; then you'd realize it was only Grandma, moving about. With Grandma upstairs, Laurie just might as well have been alone with the man.

Jules plugged in the kettle, then spooned coffee into a Peanuts mug.

'I showed this man Toby's paw,' Laurie was saying. 'I showed him where Toby cut himself.'

'I expect he found that fascinating.'

'You know what he said? He said that Toby would be running around like new just as soon as you like. He said that Toby would stop all the whining and yelping then.'

'And did he have a name, this man?'

Laurie had to consider that for a second. 'I think he said it was Mr Sands or something.'

Jules did a brief mental juggling act: Sands, sandpit, sandman. Perhaps the stranger was only in Laurie's imagination after all, like Toby's wound; or perhaps, he wondered, like the shadow who'd beckoned on Faith Street?

'No,' she decided finally. 'It was more like ... Stands. Mr Stands. He said he'd see me again. You should've been here, Jules. He was such a nice man, really he was.'

'You're right,' Jules said. 'I *should've* been here. Listen, do me a favour, Laurie. If he comes again, scat, ignore him. Your mother'd do her nut if she knew.'

Laurie was away from the table and half-way to the back door when she stopped and turned and shot Jules a look. '*You're* not going to tell her, are you? You'd spoil everything if you did.'

'Remember what I said and I won't breathe a word,' Jules replied evenly. Laurie frowned; her meanest, most impudent frown. Then she flipped open the door, running barefoot back down the garden. It looked like being a nil–nil draw.

Jules switched off the kettle and, stirring his coffee, turned back to the table. In a wash basket on the linoleum floor he noticed one of Laurie's dolls, one of those walking, talking, peeing dolls that could do almost anything except grow old. He picked up the doll with his free hand, then sat to study it at the table. Laurie had touched up the face with little red dots in felt pen. He could diagnose chickenpox at first glance. Crazy.

Crazy how much imagination you used up when you were young, making these things seem real. Years and years ago, Jules had waged entire wars with his Action Men; some he'd smeared with red paint for blood, one POW he'd tortured by coating the soldier in honey before leaving him out for the wasps. With his tiny plastic soldiers he'd staged some pretty convincing battle scenes in front of the real ones on the six o'clock news.

And, now he was too old to bother with any of that, here was Laurie playing mother to Toby and this silly little red-spotted doll. For a while these toys really came alive in your mind; strange how real they sometimes seemed.

On the back of the doll he found the cheap plastic ring attached to a length of nylon cord, and gave it a yank. As the cord withdrew, something inside the doll gave with a low purring noise, the sound of cogs turning. Without so much as a motion of her lips, the doll said, 'I am Mandy. And I'm not very well.'

Jules smiled, a sympathetic smile. He pulled again at the ring.

'I am Mandy. And I'm feeling much better, thank you.'

'You're welcome,' Jules told it, and tossed the doll back to its wash basket.

—— 3 ——

Dave Brookman said, 'So *drive*.'

Jules fought the clutch and went for the handbrake, and suddenly it seemed an eternity since the evening he'd been allowed to run his dad's car around the empty roads of the industrial estate. Apart from that one occasion, he hadn't touched a car in his life.

The engine roared like an Esso tiger; the car stood motionless; Brookman was growing impatient.

'Try putting it in gear,' he said quietly.

'Right,' Jules nodded. 'I knew there was something.'

They were in a rust-ridden late 1970s Vauxhall Chevette, which Brookman had found parked behind the Red Lion pub on the high street. The clock had more than 125,000 miles on it, the tyres were balding, and Jules was sure there was only the rust still holding it together. If they ever got caught, he would surely expire on the spot. Now he was battling it into first, coming up easily on the clutch.

'Don't forget the headlights,' Dave Brookman said.

Jules fumbled for the switch. The windscreen wipers came on. He found another. The headlights flared.

'So drive, dummy,' Brookman urged. 'Get going before the friggin' pubs turn out, will you?'

There were headlights approaching, then passing. Jules held his breath, watching them go. Not a cop car, thank God. Slowly he began to breathe out, releasing the handbrake, letting go.

The Vauxhall seized and jumped, moving forward along the street with a kangaroo hop. The exhaust went off like a gun.

'Not really the crack, is it?' Brookman said, settling in his seat. 'But who do you know in Eastfield with a Porsche? Next time we'll lift ourselves something sporty, something new –'

Next time? Jules thought. As if once at this game wasn't more than enough. He moved the Vauxhall along the high street, smoothing it out at last, running past shops with their lights out, the flatlets above with theirs on, running past illuminated bingo halls. Once, when his parents were young, Eastfield had had three local cinemas. Now there were two bingo halls. When the last of the three cinemas closed, sometime this summer, there would be three local bingo halls. Big fun.

He swung the Vauxhall left, off the high street and on to Beech Street – a hundred redbrick terraces all in a row. It was quieter here, and dimmer, its streetlights either in disrepair or murdered by kids with stones; the whole street might have been dead but for a few front windows lit by TVs. Seeing the town as it was, by night, Jules could almost understand Brookman, understand why he burned the way he did. Frustration worked its own way out of you – you either hung your head and cursed privately in silence or let it all out on a telephone box or two.

If only, he caught himself thinking, *if only something would happen.*

In the passenger seat, Brookman was twisting the cap from a half-bottle of Scotch and taking a long, hard swallow.

'You want some?'

'No thanks, not while I'm driving.'

'Go on,' Brookman insisted. 'You drive like a wimp. What you need's some fire in your blood.'

He began pushing the bottle towards Jules's mouth, pushing it hard until Jules had either to swallow or choke. He swallowed – a large hot mouthful.

'The business,' Dave Brookman said. 'I swiped it from Wallasey's off-licence. A couple of blasts of that and you're anybody's.' He paused to fish out his cigarettes, then added, 'Get your foot down, will you? You're plodding along like a Sunday driver.'

Beech Street connected with Priory Lane, and then Priory Lane crawled upwards to the Church Hill estate where Steve Harper lived. Beyond that, there was only the colliery, standing blackly mountainous above the houses like the discarded skeleton of a dinosaur. At the top of Priory Lane, Brookman leaned over and passed the bottle again.

'Take charge of this, Jules, and swop seats,' he said. 'Let me behind that wheel and I'll show you some *real* driving. Drag-car stuff.'

'Uh-oh.'

'I didn't bring you on a damn sightseeing tour, y'know.'

'All the same,' Jules said, and pulled over, 'I'd like to get home in one piece.'

Brookman laughed. It wasn't much of a laugh, more a short gasp of amusement, but enough to make Jules feel small. You're out of your class, the laugh mocked him; you can't take the pace. He pulled on the hand-brake and clambered from the car, into the amber cast of streetlights. Brookman was already out and sitting on the bonnet, a lighted cigarette jutting from his mouth, one boot-heel working back and forth against the paintwork, kicking off chips of rust. The Vauxhall looked to Jules as though it had seen a thousand accidents; one sharp shock and it could topple apart like a house of cards.

Then he looked up beyond Church Hill to the outline of Eastfield colliery. Even at this distance, the hulking shapes of the mineworkings filled Jules with a kind of dread. *Like the ruins of a haunted castle*, he thought, and then wondered why he should think such a thing.

Ten or twelve years ago – his father would have known exactly when – an underground shaft there had flooded, trapping and killing a good dozen face-workers, probably more. Most of the bodies had never been recovered; they were still down there, somewhere, gone forever, dust to dust. The place had a history of accidents, many of them serious. But never serious enough, it seemed, to close the mine. In the end they'd only done that because the place was losing money; and now that they had closed it down the colliery seemed to Jules the largest, weirdest tombstone ever erected.

Brookman had finished his cigarette now and was crushing it under a heel. He crossed to the driver's side and gave Jules a push.

'You planning to stand here all night?'

'No. Sorry. Just thinking,' Jules said, circling around to the passenger side.

'That's the difference between me and you,' Brookman said, with a note of sarcasm. 'You think and I do. All that thinking's going to get you is a bagful of GCSEs and a few years stuck on the YTS. Take a seat and enjoy the ride, Jules.'

Not speaking – there seemed no point in arguing – Jules carried the whisky bottle into the car, slammed the door, pulled on the seat-belt. His head was beginning to whirr and fuzz, and he took another sip of the Scotch in the hope that that might clear it, though he knew it would only make things worse.

Suddenly he began to think of what he was doing – drinking, driving around, under-age, driving around in a stolen vehicle, gulping Scotch from a stolen bottle – not even wanting to, not really. There was perhaps a kind of thrill to it all, but beneath that there was also terror, and the terror was mightier. If his parents found out about this he'd be in for the chop; if the cops found out, well, that would put him right up the creek without a paddle.

But Brookman was pressing down on the accelerator and having the time of his life and all but baying at the moon, and now he knew there was no turning back, no way out of this ghost-ride unless the Vauxhall broke down or . . . or worse. He managed one last mouthful of Scotch before Brookman took off, hoping the booze would soothe his nerves.

Lights flared before him, racing from one side of the windscreen to the other, blooming out of the darkness towards them. Something shrieked close by, the shriek of a cat – it took a moment before Jules registered the noise of the Vauxhall's tyres complaining. Brookman was taking a sharp bend in fourth, accelerating, stabbing with his foot, gasping laughter to the air as if the danger was all that mattered; and if the lunatic crashed, Jules thought, he'd probably laugh at that, too.

Brookman rounded the corner on to the straight, a narrow estate road at the mouth of Church Hill in which cars were double-parked, forcing lower gears, lower speeds. Brookman must have been doing fifty, possibly sixty, when the other set of headlights appeared out of nothing, veering straight for them.

Uh-oh, Jules thought. *Take me now, Death, take me now.*

He heard himself coughing up words. 'The brakes! Go for the brakes! Go for the –'

'Screw the brakes,' Brookman cried, and pulled hard on the wheel. The other car must have stopped because now its horn was howling throaty as a fog-warning and its driver was screaming abuse and the collision still hadn't come. Brookman, madly, was still tearing the Vauxhall along at a clip, only now he was doing it on the pavement.

'You know what they say about keeping death off the roads,' he said. 'See how I twisted her through that gap?'

Jules closed his eyes, masking them with his hands as if that might protect him. For a while he listened to the engine's rage, the still-blaring horn behind them, further away, now further away still. When he dared to look again, he felt he was waking from a dream, for they were out of Church Hill and back on Priory Lane. The whirring inside his head had increased, and that was partly the fear of sudden death, partly the drink. The lights at the lower end of Priory Lane were blotchy and softened, weak blobs of watercolour yellow, and the town appeared darkly muddy, not focused.

But wasn't there something else? Something he couldn't quite put his finger on? Again, it might've been the booze in his blood, but everything seemed to have slowed, his heart-rate, his breathing, even Brookman's damn driving. He glanced across at the speedo, which showed a nice even fifty-five. He glanced at the amber streetlights, blurring as they passed. Everything moved in slow motion; he tried to shake off the illusion, but there it was all the same – a feeling of something . . . not right.

Jules was rolling down a window to let in the air – maybe the air would help snap him out of it – when Brookman turned towards him, his grin gone.

'Do you feel it too?' Brookman asked. 'Car feels smoother, or something. Slower. Feels like we're gliding. Must be a good hundred pot-holes on this road and I can't feel *any* of them.'

Jules nodded, relieved. 'I thought I was imagining – '

'*Jules?*' And this time there was urgency in Brookman's voice, as the car swerved left towards West End Lane. 'See this?'

'See what?'

'How many miles on the clock when we picked this thing up?'

'Thousands. Over a hundred thousand.'

'Well, not anymore. See this?' He indicated the mileometer. 'Zero. Zilch. Nothing. What do you make of that?'

Jules watched the dash, feeling the onset of a shudder in his bones, a nails-across-blackboard shudder. The world slid by in slow motion.

'And get this,' Brookman went on, as they turned into West End Lane, where square-eyed windows glowered in houses, where the Lego-shaped blocks of the school were stacked like coffins. 'The gearstick's wrong.'

'Wrong? What do you mean, wrong?'

'Different.'

'Uh-oh.'

'And the clutch is keener. Feels newer.'

'What *is* this?' Jules said, but he knew Brookman was at least as bemused as himself. *The darkness*, he thought, grasping at straws, *the darkness, the drinks, and the nightlights, all conspiring to play tricks; that's all there is to it, surely that's all.*

Quickly followed by another thought, *Who're you kidding? This is . . . really happening, isn't it?*

'I tell you one thing,' Brookman said finally, 'this bloody junk-tub *is* newer. I better pull over and –'

'I'd appreciate it if you didn't refer to her as a junk-tub,' a voice intruded.

In the passenger seat, Jules did a double-take in the darkness. The voice wasn't his. The voice wasn't Brookman's. The voice was –

The radio, perhaps. Maybe the car had a radio installed in the dash and either he or Brookman had knocked it on. But it couldn't be that, because the voice was –

'Do like you said and pull over, Dave Brookman,' the voice murmured again.

The voice was behind him; he could almost feel its whispering breath on his neck. Jules half-turned to look, battling the seatbelt, knowing the last thing he wanted to see was what was there.

Seated behind him, the featureless silhouette of a man rose blackly against the rear windscreen. Though he couldn't make out the face, Jules could imagine the lips drawn back in a grimace, showing a fine spread of cool white teeth, grinning.

Brookman was slowing the car to a stop now, outside the school and opposite the lightless half-mile of waste ground. 'I'm sorry, mister,' he was saying. 'I'm sorry I said that about your car, I'm sorry we took it, we were taking it straight back, honest we were, I'm sorry –'

'No, Dave,' the shadow-man said, ever so softly, 'I don't think you're sorry. I think you're afraid, but you're not sorry.'

'Do – do I know you?' Brookman asked, his eyes on the rear-view mirror.

'No, but I know *you*, Dave Brookman. And I know *you*, Jules Dwyer, and don't you have better things to do with your time, Jules?'

Jules couldn't speak at first; there was ice in his veins now, cooling the alcohol, too many questions blocking his mind. Was the shadow-man someone he ought to know, since *he* so obviously knew Jules and Brookman? Had he been there all along, either sleeping or crouching behind them since Brookman picked out the car behind the Red Lion? Ludicrous, but it seemed that the man had manifested himself where he was, that he'd appeared out of nothing like a chainless ghost.

Jules cast a sideways glance towards Brookman. Brookman, the fearless Brookman, sat rigid as a post, holding his breath. They might have made a run for it but, since Brookman looked as frozen as Jules felt, that was out of the question.

'You're not –' Jules began, 'you're not going to do anything, are you?'

Then there was only the silence, the sound of the man's whispering breath, a grim little chuckle rising out of him; and Jules's heart beating drum-like between his ears.

'I want you out of the car, both of you,' the voice said. 'Do you think you can manage that?'

'I think it's a great idea,' Brookman enthused.

Seat-belts clicked, doors flew open, somewhere in the rush the half-bottle of whisky spun loose, exploding in the road like a water bomb; then they were out, with the shadow-man still a shadow, towering lean and tall beside his car.

Jules tried to swallow, and couldn't. He looked from Brookman to the man to the car, not believing his eyes. He should have been staring at a beaten-up Vauxhall, crawling with rust; but he saw nothing of the kind, saw instead what appeared to be a brand new, sparkling, silver grey –

'*Christ*, Jules,' Brookman gasped, 'it's a Mercedes, a bloody Merc –'

'You like it?' the man's outline said. 'Then it ought

to be treated with a little respect. She's no junk-tub, after all, you know.'

'But she *was*!' Dave Brookman cried, pointing. 'A bleedin' *Vauxhall*! Mister, am I crazy or what?'

'No, Dave, you're not crazy.'

'Then how did you do it? How'd you turn a bleedin' junk-tub into . . . into that?'

But the man stood in silence, his face upturned to the sky, his lungs taking air. Perhaps he was listening for something, though there was nothing to hear above the night air but the far-distant hum of traffic or a further distant Coke can rattling in a gutter. For a moment or two, everything stopped, waiting his reply, and at last he turned towards Brookman and grinned, 'I can do anything you want.'

'Anything?'

'Anything at all.'

After a moment's thought, Brookman said, 'Maybe you're the crazy one. Maybe we're all of us crazy.'

'If that's how you like to see it —' the man said thoughtfully, and began taking measured paces around to the driver's side. 'All the same, this *was* a Vauxhall before, and now it isn't. Right?'

'Right,' Jules agreed. 'So how'd you do it?'

No response; only a creeping grin that Jules could feel but not see. When the man had the door half open before getting in, Jules tried again.

'Whoever you are . . . who are you?'

This time the outline capsized into a laughter, a high, hoarse laughter which chilled and spread like a frost. It was a laughter Jules would hear in his sleep tonight, a laughter that followed him even as he sprinted away from the Merc and across the road towards the waste ground, a laughter still rising on the air as the Merc took off at speed behind him and rolled into blackness somewhere along West End Lane.

He never looked back for Brookman; he just kept on running, pushing himself on. Terror must have been a kind of adrenalin, because Jules was sure he'd never run at such speed in his life. There was only the lightless pool of the waste ground and the huddled ambers and yellows of Mount Temple up ahead, and that was all that mattered, outrunning the shadows, beating the dark half-mile between here and home.

He ran, not slowing, until stitch tied knots in his side and his head began pounding its blood-beat rhythm. By then, he had put the worst of it behind him – the lights on stupid Mount Temple Mount had never before glowed so warmly, or seemed so inviting, so welcoming. Gradually, very slowly at first, he found himself calming. It would take a while to adjust, and his thoughts would keep him awake and restless tonight, but at least he was home.

He moved towards Mount Temple Crescent with one hand clutching his rib-cage, legs plodding, lunatic riddles jumping in and out of his skull.

When is a Vauxhall not a Vauxhall?

When it's a . . . when it's a . . .

Jules, you must be off your box.

A few minutes later he reached the gate, fussed his back door key from a pocket, strode up the path towards the house. In the gloom, he almost went flying over something hard and metallic left out on the drive. It slid clattering off behind him. He struggled for balance, cursing beneath his breath. *Laurie! How many times does she have to be told –*

Never mind. He pushed the anger away. *You're home, Jules, you're safe. You used to leave things lying around just the same.*

Unlocking the door, he stepped into the kitchen and turned on the light – a strobing fluorescent which bothered his eyes. Still nursing his ribs, Jules crossed to the refrigerator, plucked out a bottle of milk, then poured himself a glass. Much calmer now, much better. He took one sip, then put the bottle away. There were hushed TV sounds wafting from the lounge – his father, probably, in front of a late film. He thought of popping his head round the door and saying hello, but then decided against it. If his father asked him about tonight, how could he begin to describe it? He would probably fall apart right there; he needed more time to think. Better to head straight for the sack.

At the far side of the kitchen he paused before dousing the light; paused when he noticed the cluster of reddish-brown smudges marking the linoleum between the back door and where he was standing. Any less weary, and he might have stopped to wonder why the smudges appeared so much like animal prints, the marks of a smallish mammal; he might have wondered whether their redness could be blood from a wound, trailed in and scuffed about.

In the end, the hard fluorescence piercing his vision, tiredness swept him away instead, and he killed the light.

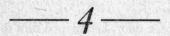

4

Then it was Friday, though at first it felt more like Monday – a double French and Physics kind of day. His bedside clock radio came on, wrenching him away from oblivion and into his usual eight o'clock stupor. Sunlight streamed in between parted curtains. For several minutes he buried himself beneath the sheets, trying to remember who he was. Before he remembered that, though, he remembered last night: the maddening drive with Brookman behind the wheel, the darkly grinning spectre in the rear seat, the hazy lights, the gleaming Mercedes.

It all seemed unreal and distant as a bad dream now, every bit as fuzzy, but in parts just as frightening. Perhaps in a week or two it would seem even further away, and then he could forget all about it. Perhaps Steve Harper would know what to make of it – after all, Steve read those mags like *Phenomenon* and *Other Worlds* and swallowed up horror and science fiction by the cartload. If Steve didn't know how to explain it, at least he'd be willing to believe it.

He turned in his narrow bed, hoping the day would spin out and pass him by without missing him. Surely one lost day wouldn't hurt. But when Kenny Rogers came crooning to his bedside, he upped and dressed in a flurry.

In the kitchen he found his mother down on all fours, scrubbing stains from the lino. She had just touched forty, a little bit greyer, a little more lined, though the years hadn't faded her looks, not yet. She pushed paper and took shorthand for a suit-and-tie job in the office at the Geest factory; that was her paid working life. Her unpaid working life she spent clearing up after Laurie and himself, forming some kind of order out of their chaos.

'Damn that dog,' she was complaining to herself when Jules came in. At first she didn't notice him. 'Look at this mess . . .'

Jules took a seat at the table; began rearranging the neatly filed cartons of cereal, weighing the pros and cons of Bran Buds, Cornflakes, Laurie's Coco Pops.

'Which dog is that?' he asked sleepily.

She looked at him, seeing him for the first time. 'Sorry, I was miles away. It's a stray that Laurie took in last night; no collar, no name tag, or anything. I told her we could only keep him on for a day or so, just until we can find him a home. *I* didn't even want him in the house, but Laurie kicked up the biggest fuss –' Finished with her floor, she broke off, and helped herself upright. 'She was so indignant I had to give in, in the end. Really didn't have the energy for a confrontation. It looks like you missed all the fun, doesn't it?'

Jules helped himself to Laurie's Coco Pops, saying nothing. *Had plenty of fun of my own*, he thought.

'Well,' his mother said, sliding in at the table, 'I

only hope to God he doesn't have fleas, that's all. You never can tell with dogs, can you though? Where they've been.'

'You realize there's no way Laurie'll give him up,' Jules observed through a mouthful of cereal. 'If he's been over the threshold she'll want to keep him.'

'We'll have to see what happens,' she said.

'You give in too easily,' he said. 'When you say that, it means you're prepared to give in.'

She smiled, pouring unsweetened juice into a small glass. 'Let me rephrase, then. We'll have to see whether we can afford to keep him. Your dad's talking about new shelving units for the garage; he's also talking about a new clutch and exhaust for his car, and a shower fitting for the bathroom. *I* need something to replace that old wreck of a Hoover and, if we can scrape it, a microwave. The stairs really ought to be carpeted; the kitchen ought to be re-tiled . . . What we really need is a new house.'

'In a new town.'

'So we'll just have to do our sums, and then we'll see what happens about that dog. Is Laurie up yet?'

Jules stopped to listen for signs – a creak, a leaden footstep; Grandma moving about. He shook his head. 'You want me to go kick her up?'

'If you would.'

Laurie was staring herself out in front of her dressing-table mirror, her small face painted with utter contentment. She didn't turn around to look when Jules came in, but watched a reflected Jules standing between green Hallowe'en witch masks and floppy-armed clowns and mascara-eyed dolls.

'Thought you were still asleep,' he said. 'What are you up to, Laurie?'

'Thinking,' she said, importantly. 'Making a wish.'

'What kind of a wish?'

'That I can keep Toby for ever and ever.'

'Amen,' Jules said, stepping further into the room. 'Toby's only a dumb toy, y'know. He isn't exactly likely to run away.'

Laurie seemed lost in thought for a moment, anxious and frowning. Then she spun, away from the mirror, to look at him.

'But he *isn't*, you see. Not anymore.'

'Isn't what?'

'Isn't a toy.'

'Laurie, honestly.' He flopped down on the foot of her bed. 'He *is* just a toy. He's got straw for guts, or foam, or whatever. You want me to cut him open and prove it?'

'Then all his bits would fall out.'

'*Straw* bits, Laurie.'

But her big wide eyes were full of reproof. 'You don't believe me, do you? You never believe me. But, Jules, I'm not making this up, really I'm not.'

'So you're not making it up,' Jules agreed. Better to back down than waste the whole morning in argument. 'Are you getting ready for school?'

'In a minute.'

'Good.' He picked himself up from the bed, started towards the door. 'By the way, where's this stray thing I was hearing about?'

The question seemed innocent enough, but as soon as it was out Laurie's frown deepened. She picked up a grinning Snoopy and hurled it at him.

'He isn't a stray, either! He isn't a toy and he isn't a stray! Why do you keep saying things like that?'

Jules could only stand there, dumbfounded.

Laurie brought her hands together with a clap, twice and again.

'Toby!' she cried. 'Toby!'

Then the snuffles, the scratching sounds.

Seconds later a raggedy terrier burst from beneath the bed, leapt, landed in her arms, his pink tongue panting. Head lolling merrily on Laurie's shoulder, he looked thoroughly at home; but when Jules reached a hand towards him, a growl arose in his throat, behind clenched teeth.

'See?' Laurie went. 'How real he is?'

'Very real,' Jules agreed. There was no denying *that* part, at least. The dog moved; the dog growled; the dog breathed. He lacked Toby's uniqueness, though; the black-button eyes, the rigid posture. He looked like any other dog.

'But he doesn't like you,' Laurie said, 'because you don't believe he's who he is.'

Jules fought to stifle a laugh. 'And who *is* he, Laurie?

'Toby, of course. See?'

She lifted one of the dog's forepaws for appraisal, lifting it ever so gently.

Jules stared in disbelief; coldness overtook him, just as it had last night, when the shadow-man first spoke behind him.

The forepaw had been neatly dressed in lint, the wrap-around bandage secured with a safety pin; a tiny rose of red from the wound had begun to seep through the dressing.

'Now will you believe me?' Laurie said. She seemed almost to fluff herself up like a bird, triumphant. 'Didn't I tell you what Mr Stands said? He said Toby would be running around as good as new in no time. And he was right, wasn't he, Jules?'

It had to be a coincidence, nothing more; you couldn't afford to believe such a thing, not if you valued your sanity. *Keep thinking the way you're thinking*, Jules thought, *and they'll lock you in the rubber bedroom and throw away the key*.

'Things like this,' he began, and now he was talking for his own benefit, not hers, 'they simply don't happen. Do you understand, Laurie? It simply isn't possible.'

She shook her head, frowning. 'Well, Mr Stands said it would happen and it did. That's all that matters, isn't it, Toby?'

In her arms, the dog poked out a length of tongue, as if in agreement.

Jules left the room, his head spinning, his argument all used up. He paused for a moment outside her door and tried to think.

Seconds later he was running.

He ran down the stairs.

He ran through the hall and into the kitchen.

He passed his mother, still at the table, then pushed out through the door to the lawn and the yellow morning, a tight little anxious knot tying itself in his stomach, half-expecting to find what he found there, outside.

The air trilled with birdsong; Jules walked cautiously towards the sandpit. Something red gleamed in the morning sun, catching his eye, and he stooped to look at it closer.

He had tripped and almost fallen over it last night, of course. He could remember the noise it made as it skidded away behind him in the dark. It looked like a trolley, a miniature four-wheeled trolley.

Only it wasn't exactly a trolley, was it? In the early yellow warmth he found himself shivering uncontrollably. The red-painted wheels were Toby's; and on mornings like this, Laurie had dragged him around the lawn for pretend-walks, guiding him along with a length of string tied on to the wheels like a leash. For fifteen years Toby had stood proud and unmoving, his feet grafted on to those wheels. He'd lasted well; he'd been through a lot.

But he wasn't there now.

—— 5 ——

Instead of taking his usual route to West End Lane, he detoured by way of the railway station and Park Estate, where Brookman lived. Brookman's was one of a number of grimy redbrick semis, each indistinguishable from the rest. But there was no reply, even after Jules had knocked three, four, five times and waited almost ten minutes in the shade on the doorstep. The curtains were drawn; the house must be asleep, or empty. Twin pints of milk stood untouched in their crate, where the delivery boy had left them; a newspaper poked from the letter-flap like a tongue.

He couldn't even be sure what had made him call. By the time he'd knocked twice, the thought of what he might say was beginning to make Jules feel foolish. After all, where could you begin? So Laurie had lost a toy dog and gained a real one, but that didn't automatic-ally mean –

It didn't mean a damn thing, bandaged paw or not, unless it meant Laurie's vivid imagination was becom-ing contagious. And suppose his mind was playing tricks on him; couldn't he have imagined last night as well? In the cold light of day, the very idea of a Vauxhall magically transformed seemed incredible, as incredible as a toy dog deserting its wheels; and there *had* been a lot of booze last night.

An Alsatian had begun to bark nearby, turning Jules timid. At once he began to feel watched; but there were no faces peering from windows when he looked, no figures flitting for cover. Finally, when he was sure no one would come to the door, he turned away, almost relieved.

Half-way through the morning's free period, he found Steve Harper outside the gym. Steve had been using his spare time wisely; he'd been studying the girls in their volleyball session through the narrow strip of glass in the gym doors when Jules clapped a hand on his shoulder, making him jump like a collared criminal. When the shock had worn off, Steve relaxed into a smile, lecherous-eyed.

'This better be important,' he said. 'Can't you see I'm researching the behavioural patterns of peer groups for Sociology?'

'Would binoculars help?'

Behind the gym doors, footwear squeaked and scuffed on a polished floor, and cries bounced off the walls; the corridor between the gym and the changing-rooms played the echoes.

'That girl of yours is in there,' Steve said. 'You know, the new girl. Are you sure you don't want to join me and compare notes?'

Jules shook his head, suddenly shy at the mention of Rachel, and cursing his own embarrassment. 'She isn't my girl, you creep. I just wanted you to hear about something that happened to me; something I can't explain.' After a moment he added, 'It's bloody well weird, if you ask me.'

'Then you came to the right person. Fire away.'

Behind them, a cry went up in the gymnasium; one of the volleyball teams must have scored, or won the match. Bracing himself, Jules told the story – the shadow-man's appearance in the rear seat, his grin like frost-bite, his laughter even worse; he told everything, feeling more and more frazzled and stupid as the tale spun out. By comparison, Steve looked enchanted. When Jules had finished, he whistled, impressed. To Jules it felt as though a long whole minute had passed before Steve said, 'I was wondering why you came in looking like the chicken that got stuffed before its time.'

'So?' Jules prompted. 'What do you make of it?'

'I don't know. This Toby business could just be coincidence. I mean, anyone could've ripped him off those wheels before you found them. Hell, when my dad put up a new garden fence, it was to stop the kids from coming on to his lawn and taking the flowers. So what happened? They took the fence!' Then he amended quietly, 'Well, some of it.'

They moved slowly along the corridor, away from the gym, Steve mulling things over, Jules counting the echoes of their steps. His palms were tacky, his head felt plugged with tissue paper.

'Still,' Steve pondered, stopping outside the changing-rooms, 'you never really know, do you?'

'Never know what?'

'Whether coincidence has anything to do with any-thing. Sometimes I'm sure there's no such thing.

Some things that happen, you just can't explain; even the scientists can't.' Suddenly thoughtful, he asked, 'Did you ever hear of the Manitou?'

'The what?'

'Manitou. I read something about it in a magazine. It's what they call a shape-changer – an old Indian spook-lore. You never heard of that?'

'No.'

'You know how Jeckyll turned into Hyde? How a vampire, if he wanted, could turn himself into a bat? Well, this is almost the same thing, except the shape-changers can project themselves into any living form . . . a crow or a bat, a cat, a wolf, an amoeba, maybe even –'

Steve's enthusiasm was usually infectious, but this time Jules was forced to ignore it. 'I'd hardly call a toy dog on a trolley a living form,' he said patiently.

'All the same, it makes you think, eh?'

'Yeah, it makes you think, Steve.'

Steve looked crestfallen. 'So you're right. Two and two doesn't make five. I'm just saying that anything's possible; I mean, you can't dismiss what you saw, can you?'

Jules couldn't, not yet. He was about to reply when the gym doors along the corridor flew open wide, and the girls came teeming out, sweatily shining, all white T-shirts and navy shorts bobbing, pumps and sneakers squeaking, faces suspicious when they saw the two boys outside their changing-room. Some of them spoke in whispers, which for some reason convinced Jules they were talking about him.

He watched the girls file languidly in through the

46

doors for a while, then looked sharply at Steve. 'Do you think it's possible this weirdo in the car is the same one who came to the house; the one Laurie called Stands?'

'Sure it's possible,' Steve said. 'Why not?'

'You don't think Laurie could have invented him?'

'Why should she? Did you invent the one in the car?'

'No, but that's different,' Jules told him. 'You know how kids are, with imaginary playmates, imaginary friends. Sometimes they make them up for company; and I just thought that Laurie –' He broke off; one of the girls had tumbled against him in her rush for the changing-room. Or perhaps she hadn't been rushing. He sensed that she'd stopped behind him, letting the other girls pass. Steve's gaze had already shifted from Jules to her; his face had altered. When Jules turned around to look, it was the new girl, Rachel, he saw standing there. Most of the others were gone.

Had she been listening? For the moment that hardly mattered. Her eyes were a deeper brown than before, her smile was silkier; in fact there was something almost too right, too proper about her, though at first he was at a loss to understand what.

'I'm sorry,' she said, her voice a pitch lower than Jules had expected, and accentless. 'I couldn't help overhearing . . .'

Jules could only return her smile; his own felt unnatural as a crack in plaster. But the new girl seemed not to notice his embarrassment, not even when he began to feel himself flush. She was looking directly at him, all but ignoring Steve Harper, and

Jules had to check back over his shoulder to see that he wasn't alone with her.

'You're Jules Dwyer, aren't you?' the girl was saying.

'That's me.' He was speaking at last, which at least was a start. 'You're Rachel. I asked around.'

'So did I.' She laughed.

Jules returned the laugh, but it came out sounding awkward; she'd finished before he'd started. And slowly the walls were closing in; already he could feel his conversation running out. Why did it always desert him when he needed it most?'

'I hope you don't think I was snooping,' she said. 'It's just that I heard you mention that man – Mr Stands. Well, I think I might know something *you'd* like to know. Take it from me, he's real enough. Did you ever meet a girl called Viv Parsons? She finished here before I came.'

'I don't think so. Did she meet Stands too?'

The girl looked about to reply, but pulled herself up short, and instead turned towards the changing-room. 'It's a busy day, and kind of a long story. Could we talk about it later?' She looked briefly at Steve, then back at Jules. 'Good. After school, then. You can buy me a coffee in town.'

There was no time for Jules to reply. By the time he'd begun fumbling for the words, she had skipped in through the door, closing it solidly behind her. When she'd gone, Steve let out an appreciative whistle.

'Now *there's* an offer you can't refuse,' he said, eyes still on the door.

'Who'd want to refuse?'

On the way to the biology class, Jules asked, 'What do you suppose she knows?'

'Who cares?' Steve's face was a map of lecherous thoughts. 'What *I'd* like to know is how you do it, Jules.'

'How I do what?'

'*That*. Those were the crummiest chat-up lines I ever heard – I mean you were *lousy*, Jules – and she *still* invited you out! How do you do it?'

This time Jules didn't have to force the smile. 'It must be a gift,' he said.

Usually, biology was fun. Even now, years later, Jules would sit on the back row of benches in D-Block (the toilet graffiti poets had re-named it H-Block) and remember the time Dave Brookman had been called upon to dissect a mouse in front of class. Hewitt, the senior science tutor, should have known better. Electing Brookman was his first mistake. Leaving the room for a customary mid-morning cigarette was his second.

Jules smirked, recalling it perfectly. He was sure he'd never forget the look on Hewitt's face when he came back to the room, to the screams of the girls, and the sight of Brookman holding aloft a full three feet of stringy mouse intestines, waggling them like a scarf above his head while he shrieked at the top of his voice, '*United! United! United!*'

Brookman had nearly been expelled for that one; he came closer still to expulsion with some of the questions he raised in the sex education classes, but the mouse was the thing they all remembered. Hewitt was still trying hard to live it down. He would have to try harder, Jules thought.

But today, biology was less fun than usual. Apart from that one flash of memory – and how long ago had that been? Three years, or more? – Jules was thinking of other things, drifting far away from the subject. While Hewitt droned, he doodled, pencilling a man's face on a free page in his notebook, not really aware he was doing it. Then he added to the sketch, a line here, a smear there, until the face became a werewolf's. Hewitt droned; Jules doodled.

He checked his watch and saw there were still thirty minutes before lunch. The hours were going to crawl by at a snail's pace before he'd see Rachel again.

Why, he wondered, would the girl of his dreams so much as look at him twice, let alone invite him downtown for coffee? For that matter, what could she know that was so important? What could any new girl know? Suddenly he felt surrounded by weirdness, as if nothing he looked at was quite as it seemed. What was happening to him? What was happening to the town?

Another fifteen or twenty minutes had gone by when he realized why she'd looked so special today, just what it was that set her apart from the other girls as she stood in her uniform whites and blues after gym and before the changing-room; she hadn't even broken sweat. After a forty-minute work-out of summer's day volleyball, who could be so perfect?

—— 6 ——

She came from out of town; that was one thing he could be sure of. But after twenty minutes, it was practically all he'd discovered about her. Rachel did most of the talking, and her talk relaxed him; she talked about things he never even thought of, trees and skies and summery scents in the air, as if they were something new. It was only when he tried to ask her about herself that she became restless and subdued. Perhaps she thought he was prying. Perhaps he was.

They sat at a wobbling formica table in a café on the high street, Rachel with a newspaper folded in front of her, Jules brushing away non-existent crumbs from his place mat. The walls were coated in grease, the air smelled of freshly-burned burgers and tobacco smoke. A transistorized U2 were singing behind steam at the self-service counter and, once in a while, something crashed in the kitchen.

'I like it here,' Rachel said, glancing about. 'I've never been in a place like this before. It has a kind of – what would you call it?'

'Character,' Jules suggested. 'You mean to tell me you don't have greasy cafés where you come from?'

'None quite like this.'

'And where did you say you were from?'

'I didn't say.' Rachel looked down at her newspaper, not reading it. 'Well, it's a small place you've probably never heard of.'

'Where?'

'Out of town.' She laughed.

Jules was beginning to wonder whether she might be playing games with him. Perhaps she came from a place even duller than Eastfield and only wanted to put it behind her, but why was she so secretive? Now she looked up from her newspaper, and Jules was surprised to find he'd been staring.

'I'm sorry,' she said. 'I don't seem to be giving much away, do I? But really, I'm not so interesting you'd want to hear all about me. Besides, that's not why we're here, is it? See how easily I get side-tracked?' Settling herself, she played a spoon through the frothing remains of her coffee. 'The girl I heard this from, she's the one you really should be talking to, not me. Her name's Viv Parsons, I think that's what she said. We met in a boutique on the main street. We must have been reaching for the same pair of jeans or something, but anyway, we ended up talking.

'I had the feeling straight away that she *wanted* someone to talk to; there was something on her mind, something that bothered her. I mean, with most people you meet it's nice weather this, nasty weather that, but not Viv. She seemed to have so much bottled up, it all came flooding out at once. She was nearly in tears.

'She started to tell me about her mother – how her mother had been in this dreadful accident; someone cut across her on the dual carriageway, and zap! – she went through the windscreen. No seatbelt. From the way Viv told it, it was a near-miracle she was still alive; by the time they'd finished in surgery she looked like a patchwork quilt, and she'd fallen into a coma. The car was a write-off.

'She stayed in her coma for almost a fortnight. Viv was visiting every day; the doctors were telling her there was no way of knowing how long it would be. I guess Viv must've been expecting the worst by then . . .'

Jules listened in silence, appalled by the story, but wondering what exactly it had to do with the man Laurie had described – or, for that matter, the grinning spook in the Vauxhall.

Rachel had lowered her voice almost to a whisper. Now she was leaning closer across the table, shutting out snoopers.

'Well,' she was saying, 'just about a week ago, her mother snapped out of that coma, and her scars began to heal. That's not unusual, is it? It happens all the time, people getting well and recovering.

'But, Jules, with Viv's mother everything happened *overnight*. One minute she's out of the game completely, all cuts and bruises and half dead to the world; and the next she's up and about, her scars are fading, she's joking with the nurses . . . And then Viv said something that really struck me as odd. She said, *He made it happen*.'

An awkward silence passed, broken only by the hiss of burning burgers, and for a moment Rachel looked as puzzled as Jules felt.

'Did you ask her what she meant by that?' Jules asked.

Rachel gave a nod. 'Apparently, Viv had met some stranger at the station while she was waiting for her train. She was visiting the hospital. She never told him where she was going or who she was seeing, but he knew all the same. He told her her mother was fine, there was no need to worry – just came straight out with it.

'And you know what? That was the day her mother came out of the coma. Snap! – she came out from under like she was waking up from sleep. How do you explain a thing like that?'

There's no such thing as coincidence, Jules thought. He sat watching Rachel, turning things over in his mind. Then he remembered something from the night before, something which caused him to gasp aloud.

I can do anything you want.

That was what the grinning shadow-man had said, wasn't it?

Anything at all.

But there was more. Something Laurie had been saying, only this morning, the Toby look-alike caught up in her arms:

Well, Mr Stands said it would happen and it did. That's all that matters, isn't it, Toby?

Jules shuddered. There was no use trying to fight it. That would be as pointless as trying to ignore the insane thoughts he was having; something was seriously wrong here, something was going awry, and he wasn't the only one who'd witnessed it. So he hadn't been imagining things after all. Should that make him feel better or worse?

At last he said, 'I think you're right. We're talking about the same man. Did Viv see him again after that?'

Apparently she had. Within a day of Viv's meeting the stranger on the platform, her mother was discharged from hospital. It was, the doctors had said, an astonishing recovery, a mystery; no one had seen anything like it before.

Then, on the way home, Viv's mother confided something which had turned Viv white; it wasn't a story she could accept or believe, only fear. While she'd been comatose in intensive care, she'd said, a man had come to visit her. A darkly smiling man, a raggedy man; but for all that a pleasant man who spoke softly and told her that soon she'd be good as new – she was on the mend. You'll see me again, he'd said, you can count on it.

And had she seen him again?

She had, within a couple of days of her discharge. Viv had been returning home from her weekly stop-by at the Job Centre; she'd left her mother among friends, enjoying one of her regular sessions of tea, scones, and chit-chat. But when Viv came in, the stranger was there too, the life and soul of the party. Perhaps her mother had secretly invited him, or perhaps he'd just turned up on the doorstep, unannounced. Either way, Viv didn't ask. She'd felt like an intruder as soon as she walked in the house. Their conversation had hushed once they knew she was there, and they hadn't invited her to join them. So what had been going on between them?

'Your guess is as good as mine,' Rachel said, leaning back in her seat. 'But you can bet it's creepy, whatever it is.'

'Why creepy?'

'Well, because Viv's mother – and her friends who were there – they all belong to the same church. It's a Spiritualist church. I don't know what they call it exactly, but –'

'There's only one Spiritualist church in town and it doesn't have a name,' Jules said. 'It's just a converted terrace house near the station, I think. So what? You think they're involving this stranger in their church?'

'I'm not sure. But I'll tell you something else I found out. Do you know who Viv's mother is? Did you ever hear of Ruth Parsons?'

'Ruth . . . Parsons.' Jules thought about it, and it sounded familiar. So were a thousand other names, though.

'She's one of those palmists,' Rachel went on. 'She's also a leader of the church, but her main thing is fortune-telling; card-reading, crystal-ball gazing, and all that. Viv says she makes a small living from it – there must be a lot of people interested in that stuff – but she also does it to raise money for the church. Whenever there's a fête, she sets up her stall and does her thing. The cash comes rolling in.'

'You've really been researching this, haven't you?' Jules smiled, impressed.

'Well, most of it I got from Viv. She's worried. Maybe she does have something to worry about too. She thinks her mother is being used by this man; she doesn't know how.' After a pause she said, 'I'm only guessing now, but . . . what's the day after tomorrow?'

'Sunday.'

She rolled her eyes. 'And I'm supposed to be the new kid in town! Yes, it's Sunday. What else?'

For a second or two Jules was lost; he could only see how the light caught her eyes when she turned her head just a fraction, and how magical it seemed when that happened, how easy it would be to drift into trance if he stared long enough . . . But then it came to him.

'Sunday's the first day of festival week,' he said, 'and the first day of the festival is –'

'Right. You don't have to be Sherlock Holmes for that one. There are posters for the fête all around school, and in most of the shop windows. Like I said I'm only guessing, but it's my bet Ruth Parsons'll be there, and if she's there –'

'He'll be there?'

'Well, who knows? I could be wrong. But if I'm wrong, if he doesn't show up, it'll still be a pleasant day out, won't it?' She looked at Jules, and her smile broadened. 'Problem is, being a stranger in town, I don't have anyone to go with.'

'It's a deal!' Jules cried.

Rachel laughed.

Five minutes later she left. Watching her go, Jules felt pleasantly giddy, as though he'd just stepped down from a roller-coaster ride. She was the one who'd been doing the chasing, not him. All he'd had to do was sit there and wait for Rachel to do the asking; just like a wish come true.

And all because of the stranger, he thought. If not for that, if the stranger hadn't reached both of them one way or another, he and Rachel probably wouldn't be talking yet. He would still be watching her from a distance, lovesick and terrified. For the first time, he felt almost grateful for the stranger.

In her hurry for home, Rachel had forgotten her newspaper. It was still neatly folded on the table-top where she'd left it. When he was ready to leave, Jules collected the paper and shoved it down into his deepest jacket pocket. He could always return it to her on Sunday.

He made his way out of the greasy café and walked home, hoping that nothing more had happened while he'd been away.

—— 7 ——

At the top of the stairs a stooping figure emerged from a doorway, so quiet that Jules almost collided with it. A hand snatched his wrist, and he saw how the knuckles stood out, how slim and bony the fingers were; the skin was pale and mottled. When the figure spoke to him, its voice seemed little more than an animal croak.

'Yon forecaster's moles are restless,' the voice explained. 'I heard it on the wireless. Seasons are changing, young fella.'

'Hi Gran,' Jules said. 'Is that what they say?'

'Aye. I been setting and thinking about it, and I know they're right. Something's changing. It's in the air. I can feel it coming, you know.'

'You could be right,' Jules agreed, trying to free himself of her grip. Sometimes you really couldn't tell what Grandma was talking about, but when she spoke you listened anyway. A good listener was all she expected, and it didn't seem too much to ask.

'You've been to school?' she asked.

'Yes.'

'And now you've come home again?'

'How did you guess?'

She'd become slightly dithery in her old age; you had to make allowances. Now she released him, began shuffling off across the landing towards the bathroom.

'Wish I could still be out and about,' she said. 'What I'd really like'd be a change of scenery, see a few new faces. It's not so much fun being by yourself the day-long, everyone workin' and schoolin'.'

'We'll have to see if we can arrange something,' Jules called after her. 'I'll have a word with Dad. We could get you on a day-trip or something.'

But perhaps Grandma hadn't heard him, for now she was grunting, 'Remember what I told you. Seasons are changing; it's like to be a queer summer, this one. I hope it doesn't go to me bones, that's all.'

The bathroom door swung closed behind her.

At times, Jules could only feel sorry for her. She must feel cooped up whenever the family were out, and no one had really given her the company she needed. The best thing for her would be people her own age, people who could give her all the time in the world. His mother tried hard, of course – she was devoted – but it must be a strain, holding down a nine-to-five and looking after Grandma the rest of the time. But Grandma was part of the family now; what else could you do?

Before he went to his own room, he checked Laurie's. There was no sign of her, though her school would have finished almost two hours ago. Perhaps she'd gone with her mother for a spree of last-minute shopping before the high street closed.

The first thing he noticed as he peered round the door was Laurie's walking-talking-peeing doll, the one with the chickenpox make-up. She'd retrieved it from the wash basket, and now it sat squarely on her bed, the dull plastic eyes glimmering slightly in the light from the half-curtained windows. Its hands were outstretched as if reaching for something, and for some reason he almost expected to hear the doll speak. It didn't, of course.

He was about to push the door to when he first became aware of the breathing. He stopped himself against the door-jamb and looked more closely around the room. Dolls and stuffed toys littered the furniture, but there was no sign of movement. Was Laurie in there after all, hiding from him? Net curtains puffed out from the window, blown by a breeze, and specks of dust hovered in the air. He could still hear the breathing sounds, if that was what they were, and now he was sure they were coming from under the bed.

'Laurie?'

At first there was silence. Then, just the slightest of sounds, a dull, small scraping over carpet. He tried again.

'Laurie?'

But it wasn't Laurie under the bed; it was the stray. He should have guessed straight away, but once the dog began to growl he knew for certain. Still, it didn't come out to look at him; and he didn't bother to wait for it. He closed the door and went back to his own room.

Hearing Grandma's quiet, unmistakable movements about the house had never bothered him; he'd grown used to her creaks and groans. But for one reason or another, he didn't like the idea of having that dog and its sounds in the place. He didn't like the idea of that at all.

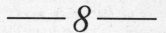

8

That night, a new moon beamed. Jules slept. Jules dreamed. Clouds passed blackly across the sky, shutting out the light over Eastfield.

He didn't know how long the journey by car had lasted, but already it seemed eternal. The roads were narrower, darker than he remembered – someone had turned off the streetlights, though the cats' eyes still shone dimly ahead in a dotted line. But where were the houselights? Surely the cluster of buildings in the town should be visible, even so late. And where were those noises coming from? Thicker and denser than the din of factories. He felt as though he were travelling through a tunnelled cave.

Who was driving?

Beside him, Rachel let out a worry-whimper, a quiet little sigh. She gripped his hand more firmly. The heavy noise of machinery increased, rattling, groaning.

'Where are we going?' Rachel asked.

'I don't know,' Jules told her, 'but wherever it is, I'm not in a hurry to get there . . .'

The darkness had closed in, so solid you could

almost reach out and grab a handful. It was like being on one of those ghost-train rides in Blackpool or Scarborough, where everything was over before you knew where you were; but here there was no end to it, only blackness fleeing towards greater blackness.

And the noise of machinery wasn't up ahead, as Jules had imagined. It came from the vehicle they were travelling in – a screech and clatter of metal on metal. So this couldn't be a car after all; it must be a kind of carriage, or train section.

In front of him, Jules could just pick out the shape of the driver, but it was nothing more than a silhouette. Even the vehicle's headlights burned as dim as candles.

'What do you think you're doing?' Jules protested. 'Stop this crate *now* and let us out!'

But the driver paid no attention. Perhaps the words couldn't reach him through the noise.

'Didn't you hear what he said?' Rachel put in. Her fingers were squeezing so hard now that Jules's hand felt numb. 'It's so noisy and so uncomfortable in here! If you don't let us out this minute –'

'Who do you think you are, anyway?' Jules added.

Then the driver turned to look, and the light struck them.

His name was Stands, because when he'd turned fully it was the grinning shadow-man Jules saw. And there was something hideously wrong with him.

'Well then, who do *you* think I am?' he said.

Above his face, most of which fell into shadow, a third eye glared with a harsh white light, bright enough to makes Jules squint. Jules could feel himself wanting to scream, but he managed to stifle it just in time; instead it was Rachel's cry he heard, echoing off in the darkness. It was as if a hole had appeared in the driver's forehead, the pale ghostly light burning behind it. Then he tilted his head, just a little, so that Jules could distinguish the face beneath the third eye; and it was no kind of face at all, not really, not like any face Jules had seen before, or would want to see again. It was more like a living, grinning skull-mask. It was the face of a ghost-ride monster come to life.

The shadow-man laughed. A hundred laughs just like his came echoing after.

When the echoes had faded Rachel said softly, 'Would you please let us off? We want to be out of here –'

'We don't want to go where you're going,' Jules complained.

'Are you going to whimper and whine all night?' the shadow-man said. 'Are you finished complaining? Didn't I give you what you wanted?'

'So far you haven't given me anything but the creeps.'

'Not true, Jules, not true. Weren't you bored and depressed with life in this town just a few days ago? Weren't you hoping for change? Isn't that what everyone in town really wants, deep down in their hearts? Well, I'm the one, Jules. I'm the one who's turning the tide.'

For several seconds Jules was speechless. The noise of churning machinery deafened his mind. He managed a glance towards Rachel, but couldn't find her face in the dark; could only feel her hand grasping his.

At last he said, 'There's nothing you could give me I'd want to keep.'

'Sometimes', the driver replied whisperingly, 'you have to think quite carefully about those things. I might have given you things you *do* want; things you don't even know about.' He turned his head slightly away, and now the light was blinding, suffocating. 'You don't appreciate what I'm doing, that's all. Just look at your town, Jules. All it is, is a no-go zone. It's dying. There's only one thing to do with a place like this, and that's burn it, raze it to the ground, bury it. Unless –'

'Unless what?'

'Unless I do something else with it. Believe me, Jules, I can make this town thrive again; I can re-make it, if that's what people really want. And no one wants to see it die and fade out, do they?' Again, the driver's grin came creeping up like a draught. 'And I'll tell you something more. Everything you've seen so far – it's nothing. I haven't even started yet!'

The darkness felt thicker than quicksand now. Darkness was all there was; darkness and the pressure of Rachel's hand, and the clattering motions of the vehicle.

'You're off your head,' Jules cried. 'No one would ever go along with you! No one wants you here!'

But the shadow-man's laughter was mocking. 'Is that what you think? Then look around you, Jules; look around you!'

Jules strained his eyes to look, and the laughter soared, mocking him.

He tried to scream, but his lungs seized with fear.

There must have been ten or fifteen of them, riding with him huddled in the darkness; it was impossible to tell how many. They glowered back at him, ten or fifteen blackened shapes. Their eyes were like the driver's – bright-burning Cyclops eyes, fanning out ghost-white light, staring, staring.

'See how many there are already?' the driver was saying. 'And this is just the beginning, Jules, just the beginning!'

But Jules couldn't find a reply. He couldn't tear his eyes from the others. Because now they were moving steadily towards him, clawing their way through the carriages, moving slyly and silently closer. The lights of their third-eyes flared; the noise was becoming vast, incredible, deafening; the vice on his hand squeezed tighter . . .

Jules was awake. His room was bathed in soft, cool moonlight.

Something had jolted him out of his sleep, but by the time he'd settled himself he'd forgotten what he'd dreamed. His hand felt cramped and prickled with pins and needles, and he realized he'd been lying on it. Tugging the hand from under his body, he held it free of the bedclothes and shook it until the feeling returned. A peaceful night breeze fluttered the curtains, but he hardly noticed; he was too far gone for that.

The distant grumble of a late train – or something that sounded quite like a train – soon lulled him asleep again.

9

Sunday morning, a crystal blue sky, and festival week was upon the town. It was the week everyone in Eastfield had been waiting for.

Jules was making a quiet escape through the front door when his mother's voice called him back.

'Not so fast, you, I want a word.' She was wearing her crossword-puzzled face, the one she wore last April when her employers finally gave her the raise she'd never dared hope for. 'What do you know about this?'

At the foot of the stairs, a brand-spanking-new Electrolux stood spotless.

'And this?'

On the kitchen worktop, a pristine and never-used microwave.

'Is this some kind of practical joke, because if it is, I don't find it very amusing,' she added.

At first, Jules had nothing to say. He was too distracted; his mind was on Rachel, and the fête and, more pressingly, on Stands. He stood at the kitchen doorway, hands pocketed, shrugging. 'So you've bought some new things. So what's the problem? I don't understand.'

Across the kitchen, his father was nursing his pipe and moving about in a cloud of St Bruno. 'See?' he said. 'He doesn't know any damn more than I do. I told you he wouldn't. *Now* will you believe I've nothing to do with this?'

'No. Now I'll believe you're in it together.'

'In what?' Jules asked, but his mother was crossing her arms on her chest and throwing her shoulders back.

'I suppose you expect me to believe these things just *appeared*, then; out of thin air.'

'If I've told you once –' Jules's father began, but quickly conceded, 'Oh, never mind. Believe what you like.'

'We can't afford it, for one thing. I saw your last bank statement and I know we can't. You said yourself we've too many commitments already. I know it's a nice gesture and that you were thinking of me; I appreciate that, but you should have used your common sense too.'

'Then show me the receipts.' Jules's father was aiming the stem of his pipe at her. 'Show me the papers I'm supposed to have signed and I'll take it all back where it came from; I'll even apologize.'

Jules stifled a yawn. They were playing mental games with each other, passing the buck. He had seen it before. Now his mother was relaxing slightly, obviously pleased by the gadgets, more obviously alarmed by their cost. Finally she managed a smile. 'Sometimes', she confided to Jules, 'he's impossible.'

His father was brooding over the sink, turning a tap, regulating the flow, turning it off. 'You've a nerve to complain, though,' he said, 'after all the trouble *you've* been to, installing those shelves and that workbench in the garage.'

She looked at him aghast. 'What shelves? What workbench?'

'*You* know. I can't say I'm not grateful, though. I know how many times I've mentioned they were just what we needed, but they could have waited, really they could.'

'I suppose you think you're being very clever,' Jules's mother said then, slowly turning from Jules to his father. If she'd decided they were conspiring against her, nothing on earth would convince her otherwise.

There was silence for a time, Jules watching from the doorway as she went to the table, picked up the letter rack, began pulling out and opening envelopes. 'The receipts must be here. Somewhere. They must be,' she was muttering to herself as he crossed the kitchen and stepped outdoors.

His father followed him down the sloping back garden path, resting a hand on Jules's shoulder as they reached the gate.

'What's going on with you two?' Jules wanted to know.

'Nothing you need worry about, I'm sure. She's so many pressures on her, she gets confused now and then.'

'Is that all there is to it?'

'That's all.' His father sucked thoughtfully at his pipe, which had gone out. 'She must have bought it all herself, just in a moment of weakness, and now she's feeling guilty about what she's done and she'll probably come clean in a day or two. That's the only explanation *I* can come up with,' he said. 'What do *you* know?'

As usual, they held the fête on the games fields at West End Lane. When Jules arrived the lower end of one field was already clogged with parked cars. The festivities – a bigger turn-out than he'd expected – stretched all the way from the road to the school, a riot of colours and sounds. On the soccer pitches, several athletic middle-schoolers were shinning up goalposts just for the hell of it; some hung upside down from the crossbars like bats. A local brass band, fronted by majorettes, marched up and down and around in circles, wondering where to go next. Jules half-expected to see the Union Jack, but all he got was a high-flying flag with G A L A painted across it.

Most of the crowds had gathered nearer the school. Here there were pink-faced kids and pink-eyed parents gathering round the tombola stall, besieging a seller of raffle tickets. Go try and sell them something on their doorstep, Jules thought, and they'll tell you to take a flying one at the moon. Blobs of ice-cream melted from their cones, hitting the grass like monster bird-pats. Babies too small to understand the fuss yelled their hearts out, unnoticed.

There were bookstalls selling chewed-up, spitten-out paperbacks, the kind you'd read before and the kind you'd never dream of reading; there were white-elephant stalls, selling nothing but white elephants, and others where helium balloons reached for the sky, trying to escape the children paying for them. Loud-mouths brayed, lovers whispered, and in a booth surrounded by autograph hunters, a Coronation Street celebrity sat quietly signing her name, time after time, then selling it for charity. Jules pushed calmly through the crowd, dodging a low-flying cornet, the smell of hot dogs invading his nose.

Where was Rachel? In his rush to get here, he hadn't been able to think of anything else. He hadn't even thought of his parents, or the sudden arrival at the house of all those new items, the vacuum cleaner, the microwave; and yet something about it bothered him. It had quietly nagged him all the way from home. Were his parents growing eccentric and weird, as if he hadn't enough problems already? Could Stands be playing one of his tricks? He was beginning to wonder what Stands could hope to gain from a trick like that when someone elbowed him in the ribs.

The elbow was Rachel's. He turned, surprised, one hand clutching his side, and as soon as he saw her he melted.

'Hello Jules. Did I break your heart?'

'I uh –' Realizing that was where his hand was, he dropped it at once. 'Glad you could come,' he murmured.

'Don't forget it was my idea,' she said, and leaned close towards him. He'd expected her to whisper secretly in his ear, but when she kissed his cheek his surprise turned to astonishment, and his legs to jelly.

'Sorry I forgot your newspaper,' was all he could manage, flushing.

'Oh, never mind that. Yesterday's news is today's fire, isn't that what they say?'

She was wearing a buttercup-yellow print dress,

which gently wafted in the breeze: her dark hair was swept back behind her ears, and her eyes were a chestnut-tinted dream as she looked from Jules to the sea of hands and faces in front of the stalls. Now she took him by the arm, steering him between children with chocolate chins and youths on the look-out for anything with boobs. When one of the youths whistled after Rachel, Jules wanted to turn around and slam him. He would have done, too, but the youth was built like a marine.

They were passing a stall of goldfish in plastic bags when Rachel stopped, dragging Jules aside. Suddenly she looked quite serious; she was bubbling with nervous excitement, brow pinched to a frown.

'He's here,' she said.

It took a moment to sink in. 'Stands? Where? Did you see him?'

'Not yet. He's in one of the tents. Ruth Parsons' tent by the look of it. I thought I saw Viv there too.'

They walked on, accompanied by a military drumbeat from the band. Onions hissed at the hotdog stand; kids queued, money in one hand, ice-creams or Cokes in the other. How many would be sick as dogs before lunchtime? Overhead, the sky was cloudless, perfectly blue. A gold-yellow sun was beginning to bake.

Once they'd escaped the worst of the crowd, Rachel announced suddenly, 'I've been dreaming about him, you know.'

Jules could only look at her, mystified. 'You've been –'

'Sure. Why else do you think I'd be curious? I'd like to know why I should dream about someone I never met. I mean, I never saw him the way you did, at close range. Why should I dream about him?'

After a second, Jules said, 'If you never met him, how do you know he's the one you're dreaming about?'

'I know, that's all.'

'What kind of dreams?'

But Rachel was looking away, her attention wandering. Now he was searching for memories; remembering vaguely – darkness and noise, haunting white eyes; but that was all. If he'd been dreaming too, he wasn't much good at recalling. With him, dreams were just so much sand through a sieve.

'Look!' Rachel nudged him.

Jules looked. He followed the line of her finger. Ahead, there were two well-sized tents, one red, one yellow, with about ten yards distance between them. The red tent, pitched to the right, must have been staging some kind of fine arts exhibition, judging by the very few people around it. It was the other tent which seemed to be drawing the crowds. Some were milling about in front, others were forming an orderly queue. Above the closed flaps, a tarpaulin banner boasted: AND GOD SAID LET THERE BE LIGHT, AND THERE WAS LIGHT! There were smaller notices pinned to the front of the tent, urging people to enter, urging them to pay. When the tent flaps opened, and an elderly woman made her way outside, Jules could only see darkness within.

They moved closer, weaving between bodies. A girl wearing too much make-up and smelling strongly of perfume stepped forward, and Jules thought she was coming for him until she cried, 'Rachel! Welcome to the creepshow.' She looked desperately troubled about something, and was gnawing her lower lip.

'Hello Viv,' Rachel said. 'Meet Jules; a friend of mine. He knows all about it.'

Viv shot him a brief, nervous glance, then looked at Rachel.

'Is he inside?' Rachel asked.

'You bet he is. Look at 'em all; they won't let him go. The word's getting around. You see my mother?' She turned and indicated a middle-aged woman in grey; the woman was chatting excitedly with friends. 'She's having a happy heart-attack. I never liked what she was doing at that church of hers, but I like what's happening here even less. It scares me, Rachel. It's . . . not normal, that's what. It isn't normal.'

'What's he doing in there?' Jules wanted to know.

'He's doing a lot more than just telling fortunes, that's for sure. People are coming out crying, or laughing, or what have you. Did you see that old woman who just left?' Again she pointed. 'Five minutes ago she hobbled in there on a walking stick, and look at her now.'

Jules could see the woman moving away, mingling with the crowds. She walked steadily and surely; no stick.

Then he noticed a young couple passing close by. The young woman was in tears, but the tears were joyful; she was laughing all through them.

'He said there's no need to adopt! He said there'll be no complications this time! He said I'll be pregnant in October –'

'How can he tell you a thing like that?' the husband argued. 'He's just a crank; he's fobbing you off.'

'But he *means* what he says, I *know* he does –'

Suddenly the air was buzzing with other voices, all cheering, all chanting, each with a cause to celebrate: the unemployed man who'd find work within the week, the purblind librarian throwing away her spectacles, her sight restored; the fat boy whose father would soon win the pools. *He said*, the air chimed, *he said*, *he said*, *he said* –

Viv was leading the way over to the tent. One or two kids were trying to peek in, but Ruth Parsons quickly ushered them away to join the queue. As soon as she saw Viv approaching, she came forward.

'Oh, are these friends of yours? How nice to see you all – but you'll have to queue, I'm afraid, like the others.'

'That's fine,' Rachel said. 'We don't mind at all, do we Jules?' Her look was telling him to be discreet, but Jules was already studying Ruth Parsons. A tiny pink smudge ran like a tutor's tick just above her left eye, and there were faint signs of bruising around the chin; the smudge might've been a ten- or even twenty-year permanent scar; the bruises were almost nothing. Was this all she had to show for a plunge through the windscreen? Less than one month ago?

When he realized he'd begun to stare, he said lightly, 'You seem like the most popular thing here, Mrs Parsons.'

'Oh,' she said, 'it isn't me. It's our – guest. He's a heaven-sent gift, he really is. We've never made so much money in such a short time.' Then she smiled awkwardly. 'All for the cause, you understand.'

What cause is that? he wanted to blurt out, but instead he just nodded.

'Is your guest a man of the church, then?' he asked.

Ruth Parsons faltered. 'Well, not exactly, I wouldn't say so. He's a kindred spirit, of course. And he understands people so well. In his way, he's just a bit of a good Samaritan.'

'I wouldn't say that,' Viv grumbled. 'He's more a kind of devil in disguise.'

A look passed between Viv and her mother – a kind of argument without words. Then Ruth Parsons said, 'Well, Viv and I haven't really seen eye-to-eye about him, ever since he arrived.'

'What you mean,' Viv said, 'is that *I* haven't been taken in.'

It was Rachel who stopped the row before it could start, first of all tugging at Jules's sleeve.

'I think we should take our place now,' she said. 'Nice meeting you, Ruth.'

'My pleasure, dear.'

'Catch you later,' Viv said, remaining where she was, with her mother. Perhaps the row would break out after all; Viv, at least, seemed keyed up for one. But after a moment, Ruth Parsons turned her back and walked away, towards her friends.

Safely at the back of the queue, Jules said to Rachel, 'That Viv's a bit of a mixed-up case. I never saw anyone looking so lost.'

'Is there any wonder? She's right in the middle of all this. She can't know which way to turn.'

'I know,' Jules nodded. 'She's just like me.'

'Lost and mixed-up?'

He nodded. 'And terrified.'

*

The wait went on forever. In front of them, the line shrank very gradually while queuing people idled and yawned in the heat. Some of the local musicians were now growing tired, and their anthems were beginning to run out of time, out of tune. By the time they'd waited thirty minutes, Jules was becoming restless.

After all, what was he going to say to Stands once he was in there? He could only hope he wouldn't freeze and say nothing. *You have nothing to fear but fear itself*, he thought; and that was from history. But the words were useless, they didn't help.

'It's incredible,' someone said, off to his right, 'but he knew all about me. He told me things about myself even *I* didn't know. Who is he?'

'Why do you suppose so many people are being taken in?' Rachel wondered. 'There's only you and me and Viv . . . everyone else talks as if he's a gift from God.'

Jules shook his head, baffled. His mouth had begun to run dry and his heart beat painfully fast, for they were almost at the front of the queue.

A young girl of four or five years came running out from the tent, and into the arms of her mother. The way they embraced, Jules thought, you'd imagine they hadn't seen each other in years. But he soon looked away, feeling a nervous surge in his stomach. The woman in front of him had just gone in, and he and Rachel were next.

Onlookers crowded around the tent, gawking, frowning, wondering whether to investigate. And the line was growing. Perhaps there were thirty or forty people now.

The woman in front took less than five minutes. She came out beaming, eyes upturned to the clear sky; she came with a spring to her step which hadn't been there before. When she'd entered the tent she'd been plodding like a cart-horse.

Jules watched her go, then took a first nervous step forward. His tongue felt more like a strip of gauze than a tongue. Then all at once Rachel caught hold of his arm, holding him back. He looked at her, and her eyes were glazed with sudden fear.

'I can't –' she said. 'I'm sorry, but I can't –'

He took both her hands in his. 'Why, Rachel? What's wrong?'

'I don't know. I thought I could but . . . I just can't go in there, I can't go in there and face him.'

'But the dreams you had? Don't you want to be sure? Don't you want to find out?'

'I know it's him,' she said, squeezing his fingers. 'It's just . . . I don't know, I feel wrong about this.'

After a while, he nodded. 'You'll wait here?'

'I'll wait right here in the nice warm sun.'

She still looked afraid, even now. The fear had gripped her so suddenly it might have been caused by a thought, a memory from one of her dreams popping into her head. But she tried to keep smiling, even when he turned away and approached the tent.

He took one last look at her, and then pushed away the hanging door-flaps at the entrance and stepped inside, into darkness.

—— *10* ——

Once he was in, the tent seemed larger than an aircraft hangar, but that was because of the darkness. It was much too dark for the time of day; he couldn't see what was in front of him, not even his hand in front of his face. He remembered camping with Steve Harper last summer in the Dales, and how he'd watched the sun come up through the walls of the tent; how the canvas had lighted up like a cinema screen glowing to life. Shouldn't there be light in here, with the sky so clear and bright outside?

Jules stepped forward, not sure where his feet were landing. The ground felt too moistly soft for his liking. He breathed the air, and the air was rank – making him think of old caves, old wells, things that had rotted for years and then been uncovered. But there was something else too, a sweetish orange fragrance.

'Are you there, Stands?' His voice sounded nervous and uncertain, a dead giveaway.

'Here, there and everywhere, that's me,' a voice replied.

A rustle of clothing, a snap of fingers, and then there was light. At first it crept up quite slowly. It began with a flame, a glimpse of candle, then candlestick, the light spreading slowly outwards, across the table on which the candle was placed. Jules watched, trembling – the table, a mound of fruit peelings, one hand, two hands, the light glowing and growing. There hadn't been a strike of a match; the flame had come alive at the click of fingers – fingers Jules could now relate to a hand, an arm, a face.

Slouched in a cheap wooden chair behind the table, Stands was half in shadow, half in light; half a mouth, half a nose, one narrowed eye as cold and bleak as December. His hair was thick and unbrushed, his clothing shredded. The leather cycle jacket he wore had gone through at the elbows, his jeans had gone through at the knees. He was turning a tangerine around in his hand, carefully peeling it, dropping the skin on the table in front of him. Without warning, he threw the tangerine at Jules.

'You want one?'

Jules caught it. 'No thanks.'

Stands gave a smile. 'Never mind, there's plenty more where that came from.' Still smiling, he reached up one hand, then casually plucked another out of the air. Again he began turning the fruit around in his hands, peeling it with a sharp thumb-nail. 'So, how's everything at home, Jules?'

Jules ignored the question; his heart seemed to have jumped and lodged between his ears. 'I'm with friends,' he said, 'and my friends are outside. There's still a few of us who don't trust you, Mr Stands.'

'Well, what would you like to know, Jules?'

'I'd like to know how you know my name, for one thing.'

'Oh, that? That's nothing. I know a lot of things. I even know what's in your heart right now – and no, I'm not a figment of your imagination. Everything you see is real.' He tore a segment from the peeled fruit and popped it into his half-grinning mouth. 'If you still don't believe me ask around, why don't you? Ask all the ones who've already seen me.'

The air was so thick and heavy, Jules was close to choking. He coughed into a fist, clearing his throat. Suddenly the place seemed more like a dark, hidden hole underground than a tent in the open air. At least he could still hear the band playing, the voices wailing; at least he knew which way to run if he had to.

'Where are you from?' he wanted to know. 'What do you want?'

'I'm from out of the blue,' Stands replied. 'I came from the last town, and after I'm finished in Eastfield I'll go to the next town. Someone calls me, I come. Just like a faithful dog. And it's nothing to do with what *I* want; it's what everyone else wants, isn't it?'

'Those people out there. *They* don't want you.'

'Ah, but they do. Have you seen how many are with me? And this is just the beginning, Jules, just the beginning!'

'But you're fooling them, just like you fooled my sister . . . and Ruth Parsons.'

'Listen, Jules, how can I be fooling them when everything I do is real? All I'm doing is making their wishes come true, giving them what they want. Someone wants a new car, I'll give them a new car. Someone wants money, they can have it. I can fix it so they win the football pools, if that's all they want.' He paused, pushing another segment into his mouth. 'I could turn you inside out if I put my mind to it,' he added.

'But if what you're doing is so good,' Jules demanded, 'why do I feel so bad about it?'

'Because your town is set to change, and I'm the one who's changing it. Maybe you're just like an old woman who thinks every change is for the worse. But, Jules, by the time I'm finished here people are gonna be in work again; they're gonna be living good lives. Are you sure there's nothing I can do for you?'

'You can let go of my sister for a start,' Jules said.

'That's one thing I can't do.'

'Why not?'

'Because she doesn't want me to.'

Just for a second, Jules's fear became sudden fury. The shadow-man was no Good Samaritan, and he wasn't here for others but for himself; the foul air might have been scented by his own scheming evil.

'Laurie's too young to know her own mind,' Jules heard himself cry. The tangerine was raised in his hand, ready to be thrown. 'You're just taking advantage of her, you freak!'

But Stands was grinning harmlessly.

The tangerine was suddenly a red hot coal in Jules's fist; he dropped it to the ground with a cry.

'Calm yourself,' Stands said, watching as Jules nursed his hand. 'There's nothing you can do to stop me, so why bother?'

After a moment Jules asked, 'Stands . . . what are you?'

'I'm everyone's dream,' Stands replied, 'and everyone's nightmare. That's what I am, Jules. Even that girl of yours is dreaming about me, isn't she? Is that why she's afraid to come in? Because I've been in her dreams, I've shown her what I can do?'

'You'd better leave her out of this,' Jules seethed, 'or I'll – I'll –'

'You'll what?' Stands laughed. Reaching down into darkness, he lifted a smallish knapsack on to the table, began to unfasten it. 'In any case, what would I want Rachel for? She's yours. I've more important things to attend to, what with all this preparation for the Big Day. Lot's to be seen to, lots to be –'

'Which Big Day?'

'The one that's soon coming. Let's just call it a kind of anniversary, shall we? You'll understand soon enough.' Stands had the knapsack half open now; he was chuckling to himself, as if amused by a private joke.

Jules watched him, stupefied. Which anniversary? *Whose* anniversary? Why did the spook have to talk in riddles? Suddenly he felt powerless, useless; whatever he could say or do, Stands was controlling the situation. He wanted to turn and run, but his legs were jelly. The pain in his hand was killing him.

Then he said quietly, 'We're going to stop you. Whatever it takes, we're going to stop you.'

Stands looked up, amused. Half his grin fell into shadow; his one gleaming eye was a blackened star.

'How?'

'I – I don't know. If there's a way, we'll find it.'

'Start looking.' He went back to his knapsack.

There was nothing more for Jules to say. Sullenly, he turned to go back the way he'd come. A very fine pencil-line of light told him where the tent-flaps were, and he moved towards them. He'd been here long enough and he now felt drained and confused. All he could think of was being outside again, with Rachel, and the terrible-wonderful noise of the band. Behind him Stands was saying, 'Give my regards to Laurie — and your folks, of course. I'll have to be off now, Jules. That's enough for one day.'

'They're not going to let you go,' Jules said. 'There must be fifty or sixty people out there, waiting on you.'

'They can wait; their time will come.'

Stands opened the knapsack.

A double-clap of thunder sounded overhead, so close it might have been perched on the tent's roof. Groaning, it faded and rolled off into the distance. Almost at once another followed. And another.

Jules listened to the thunder, hearing it tail off, hearing it crash once again — closer, closer. Surely this couldn't be what he was thinking. It couldn't be Stands who'd done this, even though the thunder had started the instant he opened his bag; no one could do that, no one . . . It was a mad, ridiculous thought, and he tried to force it away. Then he became aware of the darkened sides of the tent pressing and sighing about him. This time it wasn't his fear that made him shiver, but a draught of cool air. More than a draught.

The wind — a wind out of nowhere — was rising, racing itself across fields and through trees, tearing open the flaps of the tent as the light flooded everywhere, falling on everything. The flaps thrashed at his face, almost blinding him. The band had stopped playing. People were running. Dull greyish light filled the tent.

Jules looked behind him and gasped aloud. The flame had blown out.

No candle.

No Stands.

Even so, it was Stands's laughter he heard now, rising and falling, carried away on the wind. But there was no sign of him; only the chair in which he'd sat, only an empty table – empty except for the pile of peelings. The wind screamed; the peelings scattered like birds. Overhead, thunder clapped.

Jules ran outside.

Under the charcoal sky, people were running in all directions, trying to avoid the storm. Some were heading at full-pelt down the fields, back to their cars. Sunday best clothes flapped and thrashed in the wind; hats went rolling across the grass, and one bald man ran blindly after his toupee, which was faster than he was. All around the fields young girls in summery dresses were screaming, afraid their outfits might leave without them.

Where had the bright sunny day gone? Where had *this* come from?

From out of the blue, Jules told himself. Just like Stands. From out of the blue.

So far the rain was only a drizzle, but soon it would be a torrent. Any minute now the clouds were going to open the floodgates and let loose, drowning the ones the wind had missed. Forked tongues of lightning danced across the sky, and for less than a split second the field was white.

Rachel had been sheltering in front of the hot-dog stand, but now she came running across, one hand gripping the hem of her dress in a tight little bunch just above the knees. Her hair thrashed across her face, and her bare arms were an alpine range of goose-bumps.

'I was going to ask you what he said,' she yelled, a very small voice in a very large wind, 'but I think this just about tells it all!'

'I can't believe what I'm seeing, I really can't,' Jules yelled back. 'Not five minutes ago –'

But Rachel stopped him. 'Better save it for the greasy caff!'

Thunder raged across the fields, and moving against the wind to the roadside was a straining effort. Banners were tearing themselves from their tents, makeshift stalls were capsizing. When Jules looked up, he saw the black-clouded sky filling with numberless helium balloons – reds, greens, yellows, blues. By the time they were over the fence by the road, the rains had begun.

They ran, not talking, just fighting for breath. There were so many motorists fleeing the fête at high speed, it was almost impossible to find a gap in the traffic. Jules looked left and right, willing someone to slow. The rain lashed down, a million bullets striking the ground. If he tried to look up now it would blind him. Then he saw the gap – only a few short car-lengths, but enough.

'Go!' Rachel cried.

They ran into the road.

The last thing Jules remembered of the fête was the shredded banner from the fortune-tent, LET THERE BE LIGHT, snagging and tearing itself on the rails of an iron fence.

*

By mid-afternoon the storm had blown itself out, leaving the sky oddly colourless and pale, and the air cool. Jules sat with Rachel for almost an hour in the greasy, tobacco-smelling café; it took more than half that time to warm up, and longer to get talking again. Later, they took a short bus ride to the local flea pit and lounged through an afternoon showing of *Terminator 2* . . . or was it *3*? The seats were hard and lumpy and smelled ancient, but at least they were out of the miserable day for two hours. Exhausted, Jules slept through half the main show while Rachel ate his share of the popcorn.

Afterwards they walked back through the cold damp air, past brown subsided terraces where chimney stacks funnelled out fumes to the clouds, and it was Rachel who spoke the words they'd both been thinking.

'You know, Jules, I really believe it was Stands who caused that to happen today. I know it sounds ridiculous, but even so –'

'I agree,' Jules said. 'It *is* ridiculous. But it's exactly the way it happened. The minute he opened that knapsack of his . . . I mean, who could do a thing like that? No one, that's who. Maybe a god, or maybe a . . .'

'Devil? Is that what you were going to say?'

'Well, yeah. Except I don't believe in any of that stuff. I'm not sure what I believe now, after today.'

'Well, I believe it was Stands,' Rachel said, slowing her pace a little. 'It was just like one of those dreams.'

Jules stopped. '*Which* one of those dreams?'

'Didn't I tell you? The one where he changes the seasons. But it wasn't exactly like today; there wasn't any thunder or rain or anything. He just, well; he made it snow. Can you believe that?' She laughed, but without much humour. 'The middle of summer and he makes it snow!'

Almost instinctively, Jules found himself gazing up at the sky as she talked. The sky looked too pale, too colourless, as if its cool whiteness were a promise and threat of –

'The thing I hate worst of all,' Rachel was saying, 'is the way he keeps putting himself in my dreams. I never even met the creep, but there he is all the same. Sometimes, it's ... like *he's* controlling them, my dreams, just showing me what he wants me to see. Just to show me how powerful he is. And all I want him to do is leave me alone! If he can find a way into your dreams and control them, what *can't* he do?'

They walked on in silence for a while, both lost in thought. Heaped on the horizon, the shadow of East-field colliery loomed above the town like Frankenstein's castle.

'In these dreams,' Jules said, 'do you ever see anything to do with an anniversary? Anything at all?'

Rachel looked at him.

'Never mind,' Jules said. 'What matters is stopping him. We've got to find a weakness, if there is one, and stop the bastard before he suckers everyone else in town.'

'How? With what? A silver bullet?'

'I was thinking more of a stake through the heart.'

Rachel laughed, and at least that was refreshing to see. Rachel laughing would cheer up even a depressive. He took her hand, she squeezed his, and they walked towards West End Lane.

They kissed their first true kiss at the foot of the waste ground, above the school and below Mount Temple; it was warm and eager and fond, and turned Jules giddy. Bliss ran down to his boots, and for the moment at least his troubles were over.

Then Rachel laughed softly. 'Just like *Gone With the Wind*,' she said. She was looking at the square half-mile of rubble and dust behind them. The light was beginning to fade, even the light in her eyes, and then she became serious, speaking quietly. 'Jules, I don't want to worry you but – don't expect too much, will you?'

Jules said nothing but watched her closely, trying to size her up.

'You and me, I mean,' she said. 'I don't think anything will come of it. I don't think I'll do you any good.'

The words were knives, of course, but he tried not to show it; he just tried to look as though he understood. Perhaps she was right anyway; she was too good, too perfect, and he'd never really deserved her, had he? She ought to be in a better town, amongst better people; a town where Stands would never reach her. Here, there was no telling what might happen.

They looked at each other in the fading light, and for a long time neither of them spoke.

—— *11* ——

Soon after midnight, a figure moved in shadows across the landing. A floorboard creaked beneath a slippered foot. It was only the tiniest creak, but in the middle of the night, with everyone asleep, even the tiny creaks were bedlam. In fact that was what had got Grandma up in the first place – just a sound, only a faint little sound, but one she was sure didn't belong in the house at this time of night.

Shivering, she pulled her cardigan more firmly about herself. So those voices on the wireless had been right after all when they said how the seasons were set to change, but she hadn't imagined it could be so sudden. Certainly the air had a winter's chill about it tonight; quite strange, that, after such a long, hot spell. And how about that storm, earlier, coming up out of nowhere? Just a summer storm, of course. Something to do with atmospherics. In Grandma's day, though, you knew when you were in summer and when you were in winter, or autumn or spring for that matter, just by looking out through the windows first thing of a morning. Behind her, the toilet cistern wheezed beyond the closed bathroom door. Even that sounded loud enough to wake the house, though no one came running. Taking care not to step on another squeaky floorboard, she went to the top of the stairs.

Perhaps the noise she'd heard had just been the sound of the house settling down for the night, as most houses did. In all of the houses Grandma had been in, walls, boards, and even switched-off lightbulbs seemed to click and sigh with relief after the day's activity. Perhaps Julian or Laurie had been prowling around for a midnight snack; but it couldn't be that – there were no lights downstairs, no lights anywhere. *You must be getting over-imaginative*, Grandma thought, *turning funny in your old age.*

She was turning away to go back to her room when she heard it again, a very light, very faint thud, the sound of something softly falling. Grandma stopped to listen. Was the sound from upstairs or down? She couldn't be sure. She hoped that no one was trying to break into the house, because that would mean waking Carol or Ted, or even Julian, who had school tomorrow or, more exactly, today. No, she'd better not risk waking them in case it was only a false alarm; better to have a quiet look for herself first.

Supporting herself on the stair-rail, she started down. She'd only taken two of the sixteen steps when a thought stopped her. What if someone was already in the house? If a burglar was moving around in one of the rooms, he wouldn't take kindly to being inter-rupted. He might be dangerous and quick, and might not give her the chance to call for help. But she was being foolish, thinking this way. She took another step, scolding herself. Burglars were people who stole into other people's houses, not yours, not this one, not with all those new-fangled locks Ted had fitted to the doors and windows. This house was safe; nothing could happen here.

The foot of the stairs and the hall were in darkness, all except for a hint of streetlight at the front door. Following the stair-rail with one hand, gripping her cardigan with the other, Grandma took another step downwards. Again she paused, hearing how secretly quiet the house seemed now she was listening.

Did Ted snore? If he did, she hadn't noticed before. But suddenly that was what she thought she could hear – a low, muffled grunting or snuffling. Very soft, very animal-like. Except this *was* a sound she'd heard before, and not during the night but during the day. And it wasn't Ted, because it wasn't coming from any of the rooms; it couldn't be coming from downstairs either, for now she was sure it was above her, on the landing, moving closer in the darkness.

She tried to swivel around and look. She had to turn carefully and not rush, because the stairs were dark and narrow, because she was only four or five steps from the top, and four or five from the top meant eleven or twelve from the bottom. But still she turned too quickly, her fingers losing the safety of the rail. Briefly she fought to find her balance, but she hadn't found it when the snuffling, greyish-brown thing shot from the darkness and out in front of her.

The first thing to go was her footing. After that, everything else followed. The stairs turned sideways; her arms beat the air, fingers clutching at nothing; and then there was only darkness, darkness and the foot of the stairs rushing up to meet her.

She landed badly, hitting too many steps on the way down. Something inside her gave with a crack – a hip or a rib; it could've been either – and hurt like fury. The last she remembered seeing was a curious upside-down picture; the shadows at the top of the stairs, one of them moving, finally settling three steps down. It was more than a shadow, though. It watched her with cold black eyes, panted with its pink small tongue. It almost seemed to be laughing at her. Why should it laugh at a time like this?

The upside-down picture faded to black and Grandma wouldn't know another thing until the moment she came round in hospital.

The houselights were on.

Jules stood at the top of the stairs, looking blearily down. Even Laurie was awake now, clutching Snoopy in front of her chest for comfort.

'Go back to your room,' he told her quietly.

'Don't want to.'

'You can't do any good.'

'But I want to see. Is Grandma hurt?'

'Yes.'

'Is she going to hospital?'

'Go back to your room, you little jerk,' he hissed, and then cursed himself. He hadn't meant it to come out like that; his nerves had made it sound cold and spiteful. 'I'm sorry,' he said.

But Laurie backed off, in tears.

Grandma was slumped in a heap at the foot of the stairs, right next to the new Electrolux vacuum cleaner. She was groaning softly, and Jules liked the sound of those groans even less than the sight of her. His mother was another heap beside Grandma, down on her knees and bowed over her. She'd been crying too. Now she raised her head and called impatiently, 'Tell them to get a move on, will you?'

Jules's father was out of sight along the hallway. 'They say there'll be one here in two minutes.'

'Tell them to hurry.'

Jules heard a clunk as the telephone was put down, then saw his father move up the hall. 'They'll be here as soon as they can. They say not to move her,' he said. 'Jules? It looks like you're in charge. When the ambulance comes, your mum and I are both going through to the hospital. Just make sure Laurie's settled before you turn in. Got that?'

Jules replied with a nod.

'Why?' his mother was saying now. 'Why did she have to go wandering round in the dark? Why didn't she put a light on?' She looked down at Grandma, sniffing back tears. 'You silly old thing. You've trouble enough moving about as it is. Why'd you have to do a daft thing like that?'

Grandma just groaned.

'You probably went and tripped over your own feet, didn't you? What made you do it? What made you –'

Jules turned away; he'd seen enough. Enough to mean little or no sleep tonight, probably. *Something* must have caused her to get up and go searching around in the night; it wasn't the kind of thing Grandma did. *Something* must have roused her curiosity enough to . . .

The answer was staring him in the face.

Laurie had gone back to her room, but she hadn't closed the door fully. She always left it slightly ajar last thing at night; it was to invite either himself or Mum or Dad to go in and spin out a made-up story before she settled. Any story would do, even when she'd heard it before.

But it wasn't the open door that bothered him. It was the thing he saw squatting silently just inside the doorway itself. More and more he was coming to think of the creature as simply the *thing*; he still couldn't bring himself to call it Toby. And there the thing sat, watching, panting, open jaws grinning. It was a grin all-too familiar; a grin to make his blood run cold.

If the dog had caused the accident, then so had Stands, in his way. Only . . . only it didn't make sense. Everyone in town had a wish coming true. Every day a new miracle – a new *dark* miracle. Ruth Parsons and her amazing recovery, Laurie and this mangy damn stray, everyone receiving something they'd wanted. So what had Grandma wished for? A set of fractured bones?

There really was no way of knowing whether the stray had made her fall. She may well have tripped over her own feet, for all he knew. But Jules didn't think so. Not when he saw the way the thing was grinning; grinning all over its chops like a smug little king-of-the-castle; grinning at him with its glistening black eyes.

He was sorely tempted to walk right up to the thing and kick it with all he'd got. Before he could turn thought into action, though, there was the sound of the ambulance out on the street, and the dog slipped neatly inside the room.

— 12 —

While the ambulance pressed on, moving as fast as it dared, Carol Dwyer sat in the rear with her head in her hands, sobbing. They'd been travelling for less than ten minutes, but already the night felt like a large dark hand that was slowly closing around her. When she looked up, all she could see was the smallish, squarish window in front of her face; the twirling blue light on top lit up the window and didn't, lit up the window and didn't.

'Don't take it so personally,' her husband whispered beside her. He put out a hand, resting it on her shoulder. 'These things happen, and there's nothing anyone can do. But she'll be fine, you'll see. I know she will.'

She looked at him through tear-blurred eyes. 'She may be fine, Ted, and if she pulls through then all I can say is Thank God. Even so, I can't help feeling responsible. As if it's all *my* doing.'

'That's ludicrous. It was no one's doing. You were asleep; we were *all* asleep.' Ted Dwyer spoke as calmly as he could, only because someone needed to be calm. 'Later, in the morning, you'll see things differently.'

'That's not what I mean.'

'Then what *do* you mean?'

Now she was watching the window again. 'I can't be sure . . . Sometimes you think things, don't you, you'd rather not think at all; but you can't stop them popping into your head. Like when you hate someone – someone you really love, but just for a second you hate them. There's nothing you can do about feeling that way, is there?' She laced her fingers together in her lap, nervously wringing her hands. 'Well, there've been times just lately when it's been hard to cope, hard to keep everything running smoothly.'

Her husband listened silently for a while. Then he shrugged. 'I suppose we all feel that way from time to time.'

'So you know how it is. But –' She looked at Grandma in the makeshift stretcher-bed, the pale face above a pale sheet. 'What with work, and keeping the house together, and looking after her as well . . . sometimes she's seemed like a burden. If I were really honest, I'd say there were times where I've wanted her off my hands. That's what I've wanted, deep down.'

They looked at each other, and Carol's eyes were dim with worry, almost fearful.

'So what are you saying?' Ted asked. 'I'm not sure I get your meaning.'

'Don't you see? I've actually *wished* her off my hands. I've wished she were someone else's responsibility. And tonight', she said, 'I've got what I wanted, don't you see?'

'I'm not sure I do. Things can't happen just because, deep down, you want them to.'

For a moment she sat rigid, staring into space,

hands fussing in her lap; and, oddly, he knew exactly what she was going to say long before she said it.

'Can't they?'

Laurie had taken the small low stool from the dressing-table and dragged it across to the window for a better view. Now she perched herself on it and stared out at the night, the pin-prick stars, feeling the cool dark air on her face. She watched and waited, humming a tune: *When you wish upon a star, makes no difference who you are –*

How much longer to wait? The ambulance that took her Mummy and Daddy and Grandma away had been gone a long time, longer than she'd expected. It must have been a long time, because Jules had been asleep almost an hour now; and half an hour before he went to bed he'd been in here, checking on her. She'd fooled him, of course; she hadn't answered when he called her name from the doorway. She'd even waited until she heard the click of his closing door before getting up, just in case he came back again. After all, there was no point in Jules missing sleep as well.

She looked back into the room and saw that the Peanuts clock at her bedside read two-twenty-some-thing; the pillow she'd put under the sheets looked quite convincing, although it might not when the light was on. She picked up Mandy from the window-sill and, cradling the doll in her arms, looked back at the stars.

Jules had been mean tonight, she thought, and she hated him for it. First, he'd said that nasty thing to her at the top of the stairs, and that was bad enough; then, when the ambulance had gone, he'd put Toby outside for the night. It wasn't a bad night, not much wind and no rain at all now, but it *was* very cold; and Toby wasn't used to being out alone on cold nights. He was used to the warmth of her room. Why did her brother hate Toby so much? It really wasn't fair, slinging him out like that. The next time she saw Jules, she'd have to remember to give him a piece of her mind.

Even now, she thought she heard Toby down below, scratching at the back door to come in. A scratch, a thud, another scratch. Perhaps she ought to go down and let him in, for his scratching would ruin the paintwork, and then he'd be in disgrace with Daddy as well as with Jules. After a few seconds, though, the scuffling noises stopped.

She wondered whether she'd have to wait and watch all night. She hoped not, because she couldn't stay awake forever; at first the cold air had helped wake her up, but now she could feel herself sagging, her lids growing heavy. If she had to wait much longer, she'd have to throw out that pillow from the bed and take its place.

'Are you tired too?' she asked Mandy. 'Do you think it'll help if we find something to eat?'

The doll's face was a pale, buttery blob in the gloom. 'I am Mandy and I want to sleep.'

Climbing down from the stool, Laurie started across the room. 'Shall I leave you here, then, while I go down? I'm famished.'

'Don't be long,' the doll said. 'I'll be waiting.'

Laurie thought it was great how Mandy had started to speak without her having to pull the nylon cord and ring anymore; she used to have only a dozen things to say, repeating them over and over, but now she came out with all kinds of things. Sometimes they talked for hours while the rest of the house slept, sharing each other's secrets.

She put the doll on the bed and went to the door. Jules had left the landing light on, which meant she could see her way clearly downstairs without having to wake him. A nice big glass of milk or a nice big sandwich might take the edge off her hunger and keep her from falling asleep. While she was down in the kitchen she could let Toby indoors, too; that would teach Jules to be so horrid. Closing her door softly behind her, she went to the stairs.

As soon as she reached the top she began to feel wrong. The air was cooler than it ought to be – even after an hour by the open window she could sense the change. In fact, it was more a gust or breeze than a spot of cool air, strong enough to send her pale blue nightdress rippling about her. Perhaps a door or a window had been left open somewhere; but Jules was supposed to have checked when he threw Toby outside. Perhaps her parents were home, because now there were movements downstairs; very careful, very soft movements, so as not to wake anyone.

She scampered downstairs to the darkened hall, her bare feet silent on the thick warm carpet. Then she was facing the kitchen; she was sure the sounds were coming from there. But even as she listened, they stopped. Just the way Toby's scratching had stopped. Mummy and Daddy wouldn't have stopped when they sensed her outside the door; they would have rushed out to meet her, arms wide, amazed she could stay awake so long.

She moved to the kitchen door and gave it a push.

The door swept open, not creaking.

So Jules must have left the back door unlocked after all; either that, or someone had come in that way. Even in the kitchen's ink-thick blackness she could see it was open, swaying to and fro in the breeze. Feeling the chill, she circled herself with both arms, and hugged. A hulking shape, luminous-eyed, moved from the shadows towards her; and a patch of darkness lifted itself from the face, exposing the features, and at long last she smiled.

'Hello, Mr Stands,' she said.

PART TWO

The Disappearance

13

So this was a time of changing seasons. In the first week of Laurie Dwyer's disappearance the mornings brought frost and chill winds; pavements slid away underfoot like bees-waxed floors; duffles and donkey jackets became the rage, and folks walked the streets with their heads down, as if they had nothing to look forward to. By mid-afternoon the winds toughened, blasting scraps of litter from gutters, ripe brown leaves from trees. Cursing under their breath, gardeners raked piles of dead leaves together for burning. Midsummer's day was still several weeks off. A freak year, they called it, nothing but a freak year.

The year of the freak, was how Jules Dwyer might have put it, whenever his thoughts turned to Stands. And his thoughts were turning to Stands almost all of the time now.

It was also a time of great weirdness. If the heat had baked down as it used to at this time of year, they might have called it summer madness or the silly season or something. But there was something dark about this, something unhealthy; at night, when the winds whistled and groaned about the houses, they came with the cry of spectres among the chimney stacks, the whistle of horrors in the eaves. When the midnight hours took hold, dark and cold and uncertain, they seemed to go on forever.

As things turned out, Laurie's disappearance that week was only one link in the chain.

At the Geest factory in Eastfield's industrial estate, Tim Jessopp had been working the Monday night shift in the cold storage area when the roof-high stack of crates fell down on him. He'd been cursing the lousy damn hours and the stinking cold and the pay, and wondering just what he had to do to get off this job when the accident happened. Later, in hospital, he claimed he'd seen a dark-smiling figure, right at the last minute before the crates came down; he said the figure had stood at the far end of the storage section, saying nothing, just smiling. Tim insisted it was the figure who'd caused those crates to fall, even when someone pointed out that the far end of the storage section was twenty or thirty yards from the accident. 'Anyway, I got the break I wanted. In fact I got several I didn't want,' he told the local reporter.

And during the local Spiritualist church's Tuesday jumble sale, Molly Richardson confessed to Ruth Parsons how she'd seen the image of her long-dead husband Paddy, standing in the street below her window only one night ago, standing in his scruffy miner's working clothes, face dusted black, as he called her outside to join him. But she hadn't gone, she said; she wasn't stupid.

And the night after Molly described all of this to Ruth Parsons, she opened her bedroom window and saw that Paddy was there again – with friends.

Then, at the Church Hill infant school, teachers were distressed when, half-way through the morning's lessons, an unkempt stranger turned up at the gates. Why had the kids all looked up at once, in all parts of the school, as if hearing a gunshot? And why had they fled from their lessons, from maths and from English, from games in the yellow canvas Wendy house, not looking back when their teachers called, but running outside across the bare, grey playground to meet the man at the gates? None of the kids had left with him; but many were cheering and smiling, and smiling so very secretly, all through the rest of the day.

The town was changing, people were changing, even as one day became the next. Some folks were joyful; some were joyless; some wandered around through the shops with the haunted eyes of lost sheep. In the Priory estate, one man slept and dreamt of the revolving summerhouse he'd always wanted for the back yard, and perhaps he'd wake to find it there; perhaps the woman on Station Lane who dreamt of the soft fur coat she longed for would wake to find one – because there one was, hanging snugly inside her wardrobe; but in his room on Mount Temple Crescent, in his cool and narrow bed, Jules Dwyer's dreams were filled with the unworldly noise of distant machines.

A rattle, a groan, a wheezing of metal on metal.

Up in the darkness above the town, something was stirring.

—— *14* ——

On Thursday, Jules took the morning off school and went with his mother to the hospital. The day was grey and frozen, and the roads were patched with ice. All the time they were driving, he felt himself wanting to tell her about Stands, but he couldn't; no one – especially not his mother – would want to hear *that* kind of story-book weirdness at a time like this. After everything else this week, it was the last thing she needed.

He didn't like the way this new twist – Laurie's disappearing act – was affecting his folks, turning them morbid and silent with fear, any more than he liked the idea of Stands rushing off in the night with his sister. And it had to be Stands – who else could it be? Each day was another day when the police search turned up nothing. Each day his parents looked a little bit greyer, a little bit paler, so that now they seemed to have put on about ten years apiece.

And it's all your fault! a quiet voice whispered inside him.

For being there asleep when they left you in charge.

For not waking up until it was over.

For ... for ... He fished around, searching for more things to blame himself with.

School was hell; nothing went into his skull this week. Voices were blurred and distant as shrieks at an indoor swimming pool, and revision was right out of the window. Exams? He might as well forget his chances, as of now. For two nights running, he'd read the same short passage in C. P. Hill about forty times, over and over, until everything went out of focus; not one word of it stuck. In the end he'd grown so restless he'd thrown the book down in disgust and marched to the bathroom for a quick hot shower. It was only as he stepped from under the shower, refreshed, himself again, that the penny dropped.

Since when did we have a shower unit?

Since when?

Come to that, since when had the flatter, squarer colour TV in the lounge been sitting where it sat, so much flatter and squarer than the old wooden box they used to watch? His parents couldn't have noticed these changes yet; or if they had, they were far too preoccupied with Laurie to dwell on them. That was why they hadn't mentioned the silent Seiko wall-clock above the mantelpiece in the lounge, where before there was only wall. And why his dad had shaved this morning with a brand new Braun – while his troubled eyes were far away, seeing nothing.

Their deepest wish now was surely the same as his own – to have Laurie back again, safe. So why was that the one wish Stands wouldn't grant? What could he possibly want of her?

Jules sat erect in the passenger seat, arms folded across his chest as he watched the road. Did they say bad news travelled in pairs or in threes? First

Grandma, then Laurie ... He couldn't remember, though he was sure it was threes. There had to be far, far worse to come yet, if Stands had his way.

The thought made him squirm.

'. . . could just be too much for her,' his mother was saying, bringing him round.

'What? Sorry?'

'I *said*, remember not to mention anything about Laurie when we're with Grandma. She may be an old battler, but news like that could be much too much for her.' Pulling at the wheel, she steered the car into the hospital grounds. 'It's too much for the rest of us as it is. She's better off not knowing.'

Jules nodded, watching her as she parked the car, a picture of efficiency. So far she'd done well to hide her feelings, but it was only a matter of time before the strain cracked her armour. He hoped it wouldn't be here, today, during visiting hours.

They crossed the car-park and entered the hospital just as the first flecks of snow began falling.

Grandma was in the geriatric ward. She'd been there since early on Monday, propped in a white bed under a window. Surprisingly, all her injuries were minor ones – a peppering of bruises, a tearing of ligaments – though the doctors wanted her until the weekend, just to be on the safe side. When they stepped into the ward and first set eyes on her she had just finished gawking from the window, and looked bright as a button.

'Snow!' she cried, as Jules followed his mother's lead and hoisted a moulded plastic chair to the bedside. 'Well, *there's* a thing! Snow in mid-summer! See what

I said, young fella?' she buzzed, looking at Jules. 'Them restless moles were right after all!'

Jules sneaked a casual glance at his mother. When was the last time he'd seen Grandma so full of it? Not for as long as his memory served. The fall must have done her good.

'I see you're none the worse for wear, anyway,' he said.

'It's good to see you looking so well,' his mother added.

'Me? I've never felt better,' Grandma said, leaning back on her mountain of pillows. 'I'll tell you what, though. It's like they say. Change is as good as a rest.'

Jules's mother inched closer to the bed, chair screeching. 'You know the doctors say –'

'Ah, hell with the doctors!' Grandma waved a dismissive hand. 'They don't know nothing, wouldn't know nothing if it crept up and bit 'em . . . They only want me till the weekend, they say.'

'Only?'

'Only. I tell 'em I'll need a good month in this place, but they don't listen, don't take an old woman serious. Another month's just what I need, I tell 'em; they don't hear a word.'

Suddenly there was confusion – in Jules's thoughts, in his mother's expression. His mother began stammering like a motor boat, 'But – but – you're sounding as if you want to be here, Mum.'

'Course I am,' Grandma beamed. 'I *like* it here. Change of scenery, a few new faces, it's done me the world of good! Sometimes,' she went on, lowering her tone like a kid with a secret, 'some of us play cards in the TV room. For money! I'd stay here forever, if they'd let me! See there? That's Mary, and that's 'Lizabeth, and that's –'

Sitting forward, she aimed a finger. Jules looked around at the ward, at the nests of white hair, the weathered faces, the gentle smiles in the beds. Some were too past it to smile or look gentle, but many were thriving, many looked fit for the outside world.

'– Martha and Joannie and Eva and Stella and Catherine and Beryl and Margaret and May –'

Finished with her introductions, Grandma slid back to her pillows looking chuffed as a kitten with catnip. 'Why, only the other day,' she said, 'I was thinking how nice a change would be; just to see a few folks as old as me, just so I'd know there were still folks as old as me.' She looked at the pair of them, Jules and his mother, and cackled. 'Course, this isn't quite what I had in mind. Funny, don't you think, how some of the things you want to happen happen – but never the way you'd expect. Anyway, it's nice of you two to come and see me.'

She watched them contentedly from the whiteness of her bed, with whiteness sailing down behind her outside the window; then after a moment's thought she added, 'Where's my darling Laurie?'

Jules could only watch, helpless, as his mother burst into tears.

─── *15* ───

There was very little said during the long drive home from hospital. Jules stared blankly out, watching the snow as it gathered on trees and slate roofs and parked cars. His mother drove in a silent trance, twice almost missing the lights on pedestrian crossings. But when they were nearer home, as she turned in at Mount Temple, approaching the house, she said, 'What's happening to us, Jules? What's happening to the family?'

He felt his heart drop; he couldn't find a reply. But it wasn't the words that bothered him – it was the look on her face when she spoke them. It was a look of such fear and such anxiety and God-knew-what-else, he was sure he'd never be able to forget it.

He was watching the regional six o'clock news – watching, but not really seeing – when the telephone rang in the hall. On Monday, when the news of Laurie first broke, the telephone started ringing, and it hadn't stopped since. Mostly the calls were from relatives, the kind who'd pass you in the street without a nod, and one or two friends and neighbours. They called with words of consolation and shock, but many of them,

Jules thought cynically, were only in it for the scam. They were the kind you wouldn't hear a peep from in years – and then, just when you'd forgotten they existed, here they came from the woodwork, rubbing their hands at the prospect of a wedding or funeral. Some of those nerds would be hard-put to tell the difference, too.

Jules got up and plodded moodily into the hall to answer the phone. His mother was there first, rushing in case it was urgent news of Laurie. When she realized it wasn't, she handed Jules the receiver.

'Steve Harper,' she said, and wandered, lost, back to the kitchen.

'Hello Jules,' Steve's voice cheered. 'How's your day been?'

'Lousy.'

'Never mind. You didn't miss much either. No one wondered where you were.'

'Nice to know how much I'm appreciated,' Jules said.

'Oh, I don't mean that – just that there wasn't any hassle. Everyone's heard about Laurie; I think they understand. In fact that's why I was calling, really, to see if you'd heard anything.'

'Nothing yet,' Jules told him despondently.

'Well listen, Jules – I was talking about this with Rachel today, and she seems convinced it's Stands. Do you think so too?'

'I'd lay odds on it.'

'So would I,' Steve said. 'Thing is, Rachel told me all you two knew about him, all you'd found out. She even told me about those dreams she's had. Everything.

I mean, snow, for Godsakes! In the middle of summer! If you and Rachel believe it, I'll believe it.' He paused for a second before going on. 'I've been thinking, though. We've all been so worried about Laurie being in danger. We've been worried in case he might want to hurt her. But what if he doesn't? What if he doesn't want to hurt her at all?'

Momentarily, Jules didn't know what to think. He studied the wall in front of his face, but found no answers there. It would be nice to believe such a thing, nice to believe that Laurie was safe; but this was Stands they were talking about, not some sweet smiling fairy godmother. He started to say something, but Steve was already ploughing ahead.

'You see, Jules, if this man Stands can do everything you say he can do, why would he want to take her with him? If he really wanted to hurt Laurie, couldn't he do that just whenever he wanted? No, I'm sure he wants her for some other reason, not to harm her.'

Jules thought about what he was hearing. Perhaps Steve was right. It all sounded logical; there might be method in the shadow-man's madness after all; in fact –

He remembered something Stands had said: *I could turn you inside out if I put my mind to it.*

So yes, there was every chance that Steve was right. It needed an outsider to see things clearly. If Stands had wanted to hurt Laurie, couldn't he have arranged it, the way he arranged Grandma's fall?

'Go on,' Jules said, suddenly intrigued.

'That's all,' Steve replied. 'It's only a possibility. But the question is, what does he want her for? Why's she so important to him?'

'And where is she? He talked about preparing for the Big Day,' Jules recalled. 'He talked about an anniversary. The creep was baiting me, but the way he was talking I'd swear it's important, and I'd swear it's to do with Eastfield. Do you think they might still be in town?'

'I think there's a chance. We have to start somewhere, so we may as well start by assuming they're local, still. That narrows things down, but it's still a needle in a haystack job.'

'So where *do* we start?'

'What I think I'll do is, tomorrow I'll go down to the library – check through the local record books, see if there's anything to find out about this anniversary business. It's not much to go on, but it's better than nothing.'

'Do you want me to lend a hand?'

'No, that's all right. I thought you'd rather go snooping with Rachel at the spook-church.'

'The what?'

'Spiritualist church. She's arranged to meet someone there straight after school tomorrow.'

At first Jules was speechless. 'Did she say who?'

'Ruth, I think the name was. Ruth something-or-other . . . Parsons. Isn't she the one who had the fortune-tent on Sunday? With Stands as the creepshow host? Anyway, that's who Rachel's meeting. I think she's just fishing, but maybe she knows something, maybe it's feminine intuition.' Steve cackled. 'I'll try to meet you both there, if I finish at the library in time. I'll probably be late if I make it at all. Do you know the address?'

Steve recited it slowly, while Jules pencilled it down in a spidery scrawl. When he'd finished, Jules said, 'I think you *like* the idea of all this, don't you? You sound pretty geared up already.'

'Well, you know me,' Steve said, and Jules could almost see the grinning face at the far end of the connection. 'Personally, I always wanted to be Sherlock Holmes or Doctor Van Helsing or someone, but my folks want me to study for a proper job.'

Jules laughed, and at least it was a relief to find he still could. Across the hall the kitchen door swung shut, and at once the laughter made him feel guilty; hearing him, his mother probably thought he didn't care. How could anyone snicker at a time like this?

They hung up, and Jules tore the address from the memo pad beside the phone, pocketed it, then went to the stairs. Did Rachel know something he didn't about Ruth Parsons; and, if so, what? Perhaps she was only curious, though. After all, Stands had been at Ruth's house, chit-chatting over tea and cucumber sandwiches; and there he'd been on Sunday, at the fête, earning her fortune-tent's fortune. What was going on between those two? Whatever it was, it had been enough to put the fear of God into Viv's face – and enough to make Rachel curious. Surely, if anyone knew anything worth telling, that person was Ruth Parsons. That was something Rachel had realized all by herself. Suddenly Jules felt like kicking himself for being so slow.

He trooped upstairs towards his room. Half-way across the landing he hesitated outside Laurie's door, listening. That was from force of habit; ever since she'd gone he'd found himself stopping at noises inside the house — noises that didn't belong. A creak or a thump which couldn't be Grandma's, a sigh of breath, the hint of a voice. Once or twice he'd flung open the door to Laurie's room, half expecting, half hoping to see her there, knowing she wouldn't be.

But I'm only checking, he told himself now as he opened the door. *I'm only checking to see that every-thing's the way it was before; I'm only checking, the way I should have checked on Sunday night, before all of this happened.*

He pushed the door open. As he did so, he sensed the faintest of movements somewhere in the room, almost as if someone or something had frozen the instant he walked in. Was Toby — the thing Laurie had called Toby — still here? He couldn't be, for Jules hadn't laid eyes on him since Laurie went missing. He'd probably gone with her. All the same, he heard himself calling, 'Toby, you in there? Are you hiding, you miserable stink-bag? Come out and see what I've got for you!'

But there was no response, nothing so much as a grunt. Nothing had changed; everything was just as it had been.

But had something changed? With a shudder, he looked around the room. Snoopy grinned from his usual place atop the dressing table; the green-faced witch stared without eyes from the spot she always occupied — a hard-backed chair just inside the door. Then his sights were on the doll, the one with the chickenpox make-up, which snuggled on one of the pillows at the bed-head. Had she been there this morning when he looked in? He was sure she hadn't. Jules stood looking at the doll, wondering. No, he was sure she'd been sitting bolt upright at the foot of the bed, the end nearest him.

He started towards the bed, intending to take a closer look, but halted. He was being foolish, thinking like this. His mother must have been in to clear up the room, putting the doll on the pillow. That was all there was to it. Toy dogs might shed their wheels to become real dogs and trip old ladies downstairs, and out-of-towners might wave their wands and bring snow in the summer, but walking, talking, peeing dolls did *not* move about by themselves; oh no, definitely not.

He was about to back off and leave the room when he noticed it again; the slightest suggestion of movement somewhere to his left. This time he caught it in a corner of his eye, a dark and very quick flickering motion. He turned to look.

The windows were open in the room, letting in a draught. No wonder he was shivering in here. All he'd seen was a shadow cast by the net curtains which moved gently in the air. Cursing himself for being so jumpy – too much weirdness *makes* you weird – he crossed to the windows and pulled them shut.

When he'd checked the locks were on he left the room, amazed by his own stupidity, his own nervousness. In fact, he *hurried* from the room; and once the door was closed safely behind him, he felt strangely relieved to be out.

16

Laurie opened her eyes, and at first she thought she'd been dreaming. She'd expected to wake in her own room, out of the dark, surrounded by all the things she liked. The curtains would be partly open, the mellow morning sun would stream in, she'd lie snugly in bed for a while, letting the room slowly focus itself.

But she wasn't there. She was still in the Dark Place; and the Dark Place was darker than any place she'd ever known. It was darker than night in the house with the lights out, darker than closing your eyes beneath the bedclothes, darker even than the closet where Mummy kept all the linen, a good place to hide if you wanted to. She knew her eyes must be wide open, since she could feel herself blinking every now and then, and her eyes were beginning to smart from the dust.

She pinched herself to make sure she was fully awake. She couldn't be dreaming, but the sting hardly bothered her at all; the coldness was numbing her arms and legs, so that soon she wouldn't be able to stand and move if she wanted to. So she kept where she was, forcing herself not to breathe too deeply because of the dust. Already her lungs felt stuffed with the dust;

hours or possibly days ago she'd had a terrible coughing fit, and the sound of her coughs had been worse than the pains in her chest. Their echoes had seemed to go on for minutes; at first they'd only irritated her, but later she'd grown afraid that the echoes might circle the darkness like living things and come back for her.

She shifted in her uncomfortable seat, trying to help the feeling back to her arms and legs. As she did so, something warm and wet moved against her cheek; Toby's tongue. She could barely feel his weight on her lap, but there he was, his small body slightly warmer than hers, because of his fur. It was good to have Toby close by, even if he hated the Dark Place as much as she did. She was sure she couldn't have managed without him. There were too many things she could smell and hear but not quite see or touch, too many things that made her afraid; dripping things, things that scuttered around in the dark, things that groaned and creaked.

Mr Stands had tricked her. He'd promised to show her a New World Rising – at least, that was what she thought he'd said. And instead he'd brought her here, to this darkest of dark places, cold and damp and choking with dust. She could almost hate him for that – and for leaving her alone so long without so much as a light to see by. But he'd promised her so many things, he'd shown her so much; she couldn't quite hate him, not yet, not until she knew why he was making her wait. He might be preparing a surprise for her, not wanting her to see it until it was good and ready. The New World Rising would probably be his surprise. She wondered how it would look when she saw it.

Still, he had no excuse for keeping her so cold and so uncomfortable. He could at least have given her a blanket. And now her stomach was groaning. Where was he? He'd told her he'd only be gone a short while. Usually he came back with her food on a plate – it was quite a strange feeling, and not one she liked, to sit and eat food she couldn't see. There was no way to be sure what you were munching until you'd munched it.

How much longer was he going to be? She held her breath, listening for him. Her chest felt heavy, and her mouth was bitter and full of dust. The air, so thick and gassy, smelled faintly of something she recognized – onions, perhaps. Did she hear footsteps? Perhaps she did – or something very like footsteps. The steps sounded softly splashy, as if someone were stomping through puddles, approaching.

They couldn't be footsteps, though; they were much too regular for that, and too far apart – some were in front of her, some were behind. Then she realized the sounds had been there all along, ever since Mr Stands brought her here. It was just that you forgot they were there after a while, you started ignoring them. It was only the constant dripping she heard now, a sound that reminded her of last year's school visit to the limestone caverns; a drip and its echo, a drip and its echo, a drip and –

A scuff of feet.

This time she heard it, and heard it clearly. There *had* been footsteps, very crafty footsteps, pretending to be other sounds, disguising themselves. But there they were, trudging in dampness, moving in darkness, drawing closer.

Were the footsteps in front of her, or behind? She wanted to run, she wanted to throw herself out of her seat and take off, but she knew at once that she couldn't. Her legs were useless in the cold, they'd never be able to carry her; and even if they could, she'd have no idea which way to run. In the dark, she might be running *towards* the footsteps by mistake.

She ought to cry out – cry out at the top of her voice for Mr Stands. *He* would know what to do, at least. But she couldn't do that either; fear had taken her voice; she was too afraid of echoes screaming back at her. Instead, she could only fasten a hand across her mouth, biting the knuckle, wishing more than ever for Mr Stands to be here.

Mr Stands *was* here.

The footsteps were his.

She couldn't see his face in the gloom, but she knew his voice: 'There there, little Laurie, did I startle you? I brought you something to eat.'

Sensing the plate go down on the seat beside her, Laurie put out a hand towards it. Something soft and warm, which might be a burger in a bun; something smoothly rounded – an apple; a chocolate bar in its wrapper.

'Eat,' he said, 'eat. It'll keep up your strength.'

'I don't like it in here, Mr Stands,' Laurie said. 'It isn't like you said it'd be. I want to go where it's warm and bright. When can I go where it's warm?'

'Soon. But first you'll have to be here for a little while longer. This place is good for you, Laurie. It's good for your imagination; and we have to get that imagination working, don't we?'

'Why?'

'Because then you'll be able to see what I promised. But you won't unless you eat and get strong, will you?'

'If I do,' Laurie said, 'if I do just like you say, what then?'

'Why, then,' Stands told her, his smile almost visible in the darkness, 'if you're really good, I'm going to ask you to make a wish.'

17

The street was deserted when Rachel arrived. All along the terraced rows the pavements were carpeted white. Doors were shut firmly against the elements, and though the snow had stopped hours ago, the heavy white sky looked ready to fall again at any time. There were no front gardens, no walls or fences, and doorsteps gave directly on to the pavement. Young trees were planted at intervals from one end of the street to the other; heavy with snow, they sprung out of the white ground like frozen fountains, nodding at Rachel as she passed.

She moved along, checking each door number against the one in her head. The Spiritualist church was 27 Moxon Street – probably the last on the right, according to her calculations, the one standing opposite a public telephone box. Beyond that there was only the main road, slanting up towards the rail station and down to the town. A slow-moving gritter passed through the gap between the houses, then out of sight to her left. A cream-coloured dog darted into the street from nowhere, lifted its leg against a lamppost, and darted back to nowhere again. When she reached the last house, Rachel stopped.

She was half an hour early. Ruth Parsons had told her to come at half-past, and it wasn't yet four. She'd hurried here a little too eagerly, with nothing to hold her back. After all, the schools had closed at lunchtime today because of the snow; all the kids had had wishes come true; and with so much time in hand she'd grown restless, finally rushing.

Now she'd arrived she felt uncertain. She could either wait for Jules or go in by herself. The house didn't look too inviting, though. One upstairs window was barricaded with wooden boards, and both downstairs ones had their roller blinds pulled down. She stood on the doorstep, stamping her feet at the cold, trying to decide. Her hands were freezing in fingerless gloves, and she clasped them together for warmth. Her breath made a stream of hot, wispy clouds. She looked at the door, with its cracked and muddied varnish, thinking about the warmth inside. Did it matter all that much if she was early? Probably not. Ruth Parsons might be into some slightly cranky things, but she'd sounded pleasant enough on the phone, even gushy, almost eager to talk. She'd even told Rachel to let herself in and not bother knocking. 'Our door's always open,' she'd said. It was strange, though, that she hadn't wondered why Rachel wanted to see her. Perhaps she already knew, or had guessed, remembering Rachel from their brief meeting outside the fortune-tent.

In the end she decided to enter. She might as well be indoors as here, standing freezing like a watchful sentry. She went to the door, but stopped before trying it. Maybe she ought to leave Jules a note, in case he came thinking *she* was late. In her coat pocket she had a small spiral-bound notebook and a pen and, fishing them out, she scribbled on the first clear page she came to:

> *Dear Jules –*
> *Smarten your tie, step right in,*
> *and come join the party!*
> *R.*

Then, ripping the page from her book, she looked for a suitable place to pin it, finally deciding it would lodge quite neatly in the letter-flap. When the note was fixed firmly in place, she tested the door-handle, turning and pushing, and the house opened up before her.

She stepped inside. The first thing she noticed was how old and how fusty the air seemed; it hit her as soon as the door was open. It was the smell of a sealed room, opened after many years, the smell of an old and neglected library overgrown with books – except there were no books here, and the place wasn't sealed but well-used. When she'd closed the door after her, the air felt even heavier, more oppressive.

She was in a kind of hallway, which looked half demolished. The white-painted walls were cracked and peeling; flakes of paint were falling off even as she looked. Almost all of the light switch sockets had been ripped out, leaving trails of sprouting wires and, above her, fallen plaster had opened up gaping holes in the ceiling. Just in front of her, a staircase climbed up to darkness, but two squat stacks of plastic seats blocked off the stairs like twin, dumb bouncers outside a club.

They looked to be defying her, warning her not to go past and upstairs, but there was no fear of that – wild horses wouldn't drag her up *those* stairs.

Now she turned to her left. There were three closed doors along the wall facing her; they looked aged and rotten, the kind of doors that in horror films would creak painfully when you tried to open them. But the first made no sound at all when she tried it, since it was locked. She moved to the second, thinking how cold the house seemed as well as how musty – no warmer, in fact, than the street. Was this where Ruth's congregation came to worship, or whatever it was they did here? The idea of all those middle-aged folks from the fête meeting here seemed spooky, unnatural. No wonder Viv would have nothing to do with them.

When she came to the second door, she stopped in front of it. Something had kept her from turning the handle and going straight in: cowardice, probably. Suddenly her thoughts were confused and cloudy, as if the atmosphere in here was making her dizzy. Had Ruth *really* been so eager to meet her? If she had, then Ruth had nothing to hide. But what if she was truly hand-in-glove with Stands, what if Stands had her under his power, what then? Couldn't they have trapped her into coming here? Rachel chewed her lip nervously, wondering.

But she couldn't afford to be timid. She needed answers – and not only for Laurie Dwyer's sake but her own. She needed to know more about the dreams; dreams that became worse each night, leaving her afraid and confused and not knowing who she was or where she was from, leaving her in terror of the things they showed her. She needed to know more of the place she'd dreamed of, the Dark Place, the worst thing her dreams had brought her so far. Because when she came to the Dark Place – that was where her dreams stopped, and stopped sharply; that was where Stands was leading her. And Stands was in the Dark Place, and so was she, and Jules was there, and Laurie? – yes, she was sure. Laurie too. And that was where it would happen. Whatever the shadow-man was planning, that was the place. She had to find out why the dreams kept taking her there, why Stands kept taking her there. Whether Ruth could be trusted or not hardly mattered at all. She had to go in; she had to open the door and go in, be bold, not afraid. She only hoped the Dark Place wasn't there on the other side of the door when she pushed it ajar.

It wasn't, but at first she thought she'd stepped into another world. As soon as she had the door half-open the air rushed at her, stinking of furniture polish, air freshener. It was dark, with both large windows covered by roller blinds, but it wasn't *that* dark, it wasn't the place of her dreams. Breathing a huge sigh of relief, she went in.

Two rooms had been knocked through into one, forming a long rectangular space. It must be the place they used as the chapel, Rachel thought, since one end of the room had a makeshift platform and lectern, a poor man's altar, and behind that a large, squarish tapestry which she couldn't quite make out in the half-light. Between the altar and the blinded windows there were several rows of moulded plastic seats, the same kind you'd find in schools and hospitals, like the ones that guarded the staircase. They sat in neat lines on a carpeted floor, empty. She couldn't see details or colours – most of the room was bathed in shadows – but she could sense how clean the place was, how well tended. It wasn't what she'd expected. After the hall outside, she would have been less surprised to step into a mouldering dungeon.

She was wondering whether to investigate further or simply sit down and wait when sudden movement caught her eye. It was off to her right, at the altar end of the room. Straining to see in the murky light, she could only just make it out. Six or eight feet along from the altar, coloured streamers hung and shifted in an open doorway. It was either a draught which moved them, or someone in the adjoining room, causing them to move.

She set off down the aisle between the chairs towards the doorway. If someone had been watching her from the next room she'd like to know why they hadn't come forward. For some reason she couldn't imagine Ruth hiding back there like a spy. There were no sounds, though, no tell-tale signs of anyone else, only the muffled pad of her own feet over the carpet.

She passed the rows of seats, and then stopped. The streamers were perfectly still, as though holding their breath, but now there was movement behind her. How had she missed it?

She spun around, hoping to see Jules or Steve Harper – or even Ruth, for that matter. Right now, any familiar face would do. But all she could see were the rows of shadows on seats; no Jules, no Steve. It was only when she looked more closely, squinting from seat to seat, that she noticed one of the shadows stirring. Only it wasn't a shadow exactly. Seated in the middle of the front row, it looked more like a hunched dark figure. Her first thought was to run from it, either back the way she'd come or towards the streamers and whatever lay beyond. But when the figure raised its head, turning its worn and worried face to look at her, she realized she couldn't move at all.

— 18 —

It was just after four as Jules turned in at Park Estate, slowing his pace from a clip to a dawdle. This was his quickest route to Moxon Street, the route he usually took to the station, but now he was beginning to wish he'd gone the long way round. He was going to be early – Rachel had told him four-thirty – and he didn't much fancy waiting alone at the spook-church until she turned up. So he dawdled along, tracing out furrows with a forefinger in the collected snow on garden walls, studying the same-looking semis with great interest as he passed, as if all of this would add time to his journey. It would, but not much.

He couldn't help thinking how much improved, how much newer the grimy redbrick houses looked today. Their paintwork wasn't the same blistered, chipped and forgotten eyesore he remembered; the spring hinges on the gates seemed cleaner, less rusted, and even the gardens looked cared for. It was probably an illusion caused by the snow, he thought. The snow gave everything a sharper, brighter appearance. A brood of dwarfish white figures on one front lawn would become garden gnomes again as soon as they thawed. Just now they looked like evil doll-sized snowmen, and all the better for it. But the real tale was told by the grey, slushy mounds which had been shovelled aside from the gateways. Already these snow-piles were turning filthy, flecked grey and black by coal-dust and soot from the atmosphere. Under the cold, white camouflage, you'd probably find Park Estate as grubbily depressing as ever.

All these observations took up more time, but still not enough. He dropped from a dawdle to a crawl, and then had to stop dead altogether as a bright red football shot out from one of the gardens in front of him. Two young boys ran after it and into the street, squawking like gulls. If a car had come then, they would've been dogmeat. They both hit the ice at once and fell laughing, watching the ball chase away.

Then, when Jules turned back and looked at the houses, he realized they'd stopped him short outside Brookman's. At first he hadn't noticed where he was, or hadn't recognized it – at the best of times all of these places looked alike. He decided he might as well see if Brookman was home, now that he was here; whatever Brookman had to say, there was no doubt left in his mind. The Vauxhall trick was peanuts. He'd seen much more since then.

The house looked as quiet as it had last week, but he approached it and knocked anyway. Was it really only a week since all of this started? That seemed incredible. So much had happened. He waited a few seconds, then knocked again. Presently he heard what he thought were movements indoors – a series of dull thumping steps, a clicking of latches, a turning of keys, a long moment's hesitation. The door slid open, inch by inch, and then stopped. A security chain held it fast, barring the way.

He almost cried out when he saw the face that confronted him. It was the face of a mole; it couldn't have seen daylight in an age. The eyes were sunken and dark, and didn't appear to see him. The hair was an unbrushed, unwashed tangle, and the chops were overgrown with peach fuzz. One hand came up, protecting the eyes from the light.

'Dave?'

For a matter of seconds, Brookman just looked at him, bewildered. Then he mumbled, 'Who are you?'

'Don't you know? Don't you know who I am?' It was either a prize of a hangover or something was badly wrong. 'Dave, this is Jules.'

'Jules?' At last, a spark of recognition. 'Jules Dwyer?'

'That's it. What the hell happened to –'

The door closed in his face. The chain clinked. The door opened wide.

'You'd better come in,' Brookman said.

Jules followed him inside to a darkened hall, and had to wait while Brookman reconnected the security chain, threw a bolt, turned a key, clicked a yale. The hall stank of grease and oil, and was littered with bits of bicycle. A wheelless frame leaned against a wall at the foot of the stairs. Brookman moved away from the door and, without speaking, led the way upstairs. He was wearing only a dressing gown and slippers. He moved in a daze like a sleepwalker. At the top of the stairs he turned right, and Jules followed him into a room that made the hall they'd just left look like an ad for *Good Housekeeping*.

Everything in here was blurred by a screen of smoke. Even the walls had a greyish look, and the air smelled of stale sweat and cigarettes, old clothes and spoiled food. The floor was a jungle of ripped and torn magazines, sleeveless records, unwashed cups and saucers. Three large ashtrays were flooded with butts, and several cigarettes had been stubbed out on the carpet, leaving black-brown scorch marks. There were crumpled cigarette packets and empty half-bottles of whisky. The sheets had been yanked from the bed and left in a heap on the floor.

'Dave, what happened?'

Brookman ignored him. He closed the bedroom door and locked it with a bolt, which looked shinily new. Then he crossed to the bedsheets and flopped down, rooting around in the rubble for a cigarette. He picked up a packet, found it was empty, and crushed it in his fist with a quiet, four-letter curse. He was still ignoring Jules who came around and sat on the bed next to him; mattress springs tweaked and twanged as Jules put his weight on the bed. Finally Brookman came up with a box of matches and a half-smoked butt with a blackened end. He lighted what was left of the cigarette, ran a hand through his hair, which was slicked and shining with grease, then turned to look at Jules.

'You got away, then,' he said.

'What?'

'That night last week. The creep in the car. You got away.'

'Oh sure,' said Jules, remembering the mad, blind dash up the waste ground, the sound of the car and crazed laughter behind him. 'I got away all right.'

Brookman nodded thoughtfully. 'I didn't.'

A long silence followed. Brookman's fingers trembled like leaves as he drew on the cigarette. It was Jules who managed to speak first.

'I thought you'd legged it. I thought you ran like hell. I –' He stopped; he hadn't *seen* Brookman run, he hadn't dared look back. All he'd been able to think of was the distance between him and West End Lane.

'I couldn't move,' Brookman muttered, 'I wanted to do like you, just scarper as fast as I could, but . . . I didn't want to get back in that car either, but he made me. He even asked me if I needed a lift and I told him *yes*. I didn't *mean* yes. It was like a bloody dream, that's what. He'd got me so I couldn't do what I wanted. He put the words in my mouth.' Leaning forward, Brookman ground out the last of his cigarette on a clear patch of carpet. 'He took me and showed me . . . showed me things I couldn't describe. He showed me the town, Jules, *this* town. And it was all changed.'

Jules shifted uneasily where he sat. 'How do you mean, changed?'

'All different. Newer. We drove through the town and saw it the way it *will* be, not the way it is. They had money to spend; they were building new houses. Shops were opening, not closing. But the people –' Dave Brookman shook his head; his eyes were avoiding Jules's. 'The people were like zombies. They weren't like living people, they were –' Again, he broke off. Sighing, he leaned back against the wall. 'I'm telling you, Jules, if I had one good wish after what he showed me, I'd wish for this town to stay as dead and as dull as it is. I don't want to see that fella again, Jules, not ever, not *ever*.'

'Is that why you're living like this?' Jules asked. 'All those locks and chains. You think that'll keep him out?'

Brookman didn't reply. Still leaning against the wall, he drew his knees up to his chin and then sat staring at nothing in particular. Jules looked at him, wondering. This wasn't Brookman, not the old Brookman. Even his eyes, normally so wild and scheming, seemed timid as the eyes of a mouse. For some reason Jules couldn't help thinking of the mouse that Brookman dissected all those years ago; but now it was Brookman who looked like the victim.

'Do your folks know about any of this?' Jules said, looking around the room.

Brookman shrugged. 'What do they care? There's nothing they can do. Ever since Ma ran out on the old fart we've all lived our own lives here.'

'Whatever he showed you last week,' Jules said, 'when he showed you the town, I think he's going to try to make it come true.'

'Try?' Brookman stiffened. 'He doesn't need to try! He can do any damn thing he wants! Believe me, I've seen. I've seen what he can do.'

'So have I. Did he show you how, or what, or when?'

'No. He was toying with me, that's all. I was just fun and games to him. But I saw as much as I wanted to see. I haven't been out of this stinking room for a week, because of him.'

'But you can't stay in here forever,' Jules said. 'What'll it be like in here in *another* week? You'll have to come out sooner or later.'

'When he leaves town. *If* he leaves town. Not
before,' Brookman said, and began once again to comb
his floor for cigarettes. He found one nestling, a little
squashed, inside an Adidas trainer. He put it to his
lips, struck a match, set it alight. 'Could you fetch me
a pack next time you come? I'm running a bit short.'
Brookman shook the match, then started to prod himself hard in the chest. 'I might be holed up in here but
I know what's going on. I've been sitting and figuring
things out for myself. I'm not stupid. I can still see
what's happening out there; I can hear what they're
saying – the old bags on their doorsteps, the kids on
their bikes. They think he's a god or something, but
he isn't. He's the bogeyman, that's what he bloody is.
I'll bet he's the one who brought the snow, isn't he?'

'I think so,' Jules said, and was about to say something more when Brookman went on –

'Ha! The snow? That's nothing. Chicken-feed. He
could raise the dead if he needed to. He could turn
you and me into dust. He could –' This time Brookman
stopped himself, as if a thought or memory had
suddenly zapped him.

'How can you know all that', Jules asked, 'when
you've been stuck in here for a week? What did he
show you that scares you so much?'

Brookman took a long nervous draw on his cigarette,
jetting out smoke from his nostrils. He tried to look at
Jules but couldn't; instead he studied his slippered
feet, shaking his head.

'He showed me his face,' he said. 'He showed me
his face and what was under his face – and, Jules, it
was a dead man's face, he whipped off his mask and

there it was underneath, with bits of it falling off and him still grinning and laughing and –' He plunged into silence. For a matter of seconds he stared at his slippers, probably not even seeing them. Then he added, 'That's why I'm not coming out.'

Jules shuffled nervously on the bed; a spring pinged. Was there something familiar in Brookman's description, something he'd seen for himself, something he'd dreamed? He struggled to remember, but it was no good, too far gone, too dim to see. If he'd seen the shadow-man's real face, it must have been in his dreams, and it hadn't stuck. Maybe he'd be better off not remembering. He watched Brookman sucking in smoke, blowing it out, sucking it in, and told him, 'You're not the only one he's got to, y'know. Some of us are out there looking for him. He's in hiding.'

'Well, let him stay in hiding, is my advice. What's there to look for, anyway? Why do you want to do a mad thing like that?'

'Because he's taken Laurie,' Jules said, and Brookman looked at him blankly. 'My kid sister,' he explained.

'Good God.'

'She's been gone since Sunday. We think they're still local, but –'

Brookman gave a dry, smoky whistle. 'You'll only find him if he wants to be found; I hope you realize that. It'll be like trying to find –'

'A needle in a haystack; I know.'

Brookman said nothing for a minute. Frowning, he stabbed out his cigarette on another free patch of carpet. Then he looked up. 'You know what I think?

Them kids, he wants 'em because they're the ones with the power. Like Laurie. They're the ones who can give him what he wants.'

Jules stared vacantly back. 'What power?'

'Well, think. You're supposed to be the thinker. The power of imagination. They imagine all kinds of things, don't they, kids, what with their play-toys, their dolls in prams, their games; I used to be like that, you probably did, we all did. Can't you remember how many times I killed you while we were playing war?'

Jules did remember. 'I killed you a few times too, except you wouldn't die. You always said it was just a scratch, and got up again.'

'But we're not like that now, are we? We don't really think about that stuff now. We only think about beer and girls and jobs and who won the bleedin' football match.'

'And maybe one or two other things,' Jules said.

'But we don't use our imagination anymore, do we? Laurie does, all those other young kids do, but we don't. That's why we're no good use to that bogeyman; he can't do much with us.' Brookman stood, brushed himself off, began to pace the room like an amateur sleuth. 'Remember last week in the car? All I wanted was a better motor than that beaten old Vauxhall; I could really imagine being in one, and I was going to have one some day, still am. But that's why he gave me a better car – and that's all he could use me for, because right then that's all I wanted. You see, Jules? You and me, we don't have imagination strong enough to interest him, not really. With adults, all they want is money and good health –'

And new Electrolux vacuum cleaners and microwave ovens and flatter, squarer TV sets, Jules thought with a shudder.

'But with the kids,' Brookman went on, 'the sky's the limit. The kids are the ones with the power because they're the ones with the wildest imaginations. It's like the ultimate sick Jim'll Fix It joke. Them kids on their new BMX bikes – half of 'em never had bikes before; but that's nothing. What they don't know is that the more they want, the more they wish for, the stronger *he* gets.'

'You're saying he increases his power by feeding off the kids,' Jules said.

Brookman nodded.

'Or anyone else with a strong imagination? Anyone else who wants a thing badly enough?'

'Could be.'

Jules was dumbfounded; suddenly his thoughts felt heavy enough to crush him. He watched as Brookman went back to his knees and scrambled, grumbling, through a quagmire of cast-off clothes, record sleeves, coffee cups, searching for yet one more link in his chain of smokes. So Stands had abducted Laurie for the power she had, the power of her imagination – and until now he'd used that power for Laurie's benefit; but what if he could use it himself? And what if the power came from others too, the ones who weren't children but imagined and believed and wanted like children? The Spiritualists, perhaps.

All at once he could see what he should have seen much sooner. It was as if Stands himself were speaking in his mind from a desolate and far-off place: *This is just the beginning, Jules, just the beginning!* So far he'd been staring at the tip of an iceberg, at the signs and wonders before the real changes took place; but what of the iceberg itself?

Later, when he walked from the house and on through Park Estate, he could still hear Dave Brookman's words repeating inside his head, time and again, a record stuck in the groove: *He could raise the dead if he needed to . . . He could turn you and me into dust . . .*

Jules kicked snow from the pavement, and speeded his walk from a dawdle to a clip. It wasn't the most reassuring thought to have spinning through your mind as you moved, still a few minutes early, towards Moxon Street and the Spiritualist church.

—— *19* ——

'I'm sorry if I startled you,' Ruth Parsons said. 'I must've given you quite a turn back there.'

'I'm just a little jumpy,' Rachel replied. 'Getting jumpier all the time. Anyway, I shouldn't have been prowling about like that. I should've knocked or called. I'm sorry if I interrupted – anything.'

'No, that's perfectly all right. I was praying for guidance.' Ruth turned off the kettle, put tea bags into mugs, added boiling water, milk and sugar, and stirred. She looked like she'd gained twenty years. Her bruises had faded, the pinkish scar above her eye had gone completely, but now she seemed almost grey with worry. Her colour had drained, and her brow was a relief map of wrinkles. Rachel had been so shocked by the change in her, she hadn't been able to speak for minutes; she'd frozen as if a ghost had brushed past her. Now, at last, her nerves were beginning to settle.

She sat at the kitchen table, between the streamers and the worktop where Ruth stirred the teas in front of a large venetian-blinded window. Like the chapel, the kitchen had been cared for. The furniture was newish, with a look of formica and much scrubbing; the ceiling had only recently been painted; in one corner she saw a two-ring burner with an oven beneath it, in another an electric toaster – all the things you might want for a cosy after-sermon supper. Only the table at which she sat looked forgotten. It was flecked with yesterday's cake crumbs. A fat pack of Tarot cards sat face-down in the centre of the table, as if ashamed or afraid to show themselves. Next to the cards, a pocket-sized Bible had been left open at a page, and Rachel noticed how a couple of lines had been underlined in red. She had to cock her head to one side to see what was there, but before she could read it, Ruth set her tea-mug on the table with a slight thump.

Rachel thanked her, and waited for Ruth to pull up a chair. 'You were saying about praying for guidance. Is it a god you people pray to, or what?'

Ruth's mouth smiled, though her eyes didn't. 'The same God as everyone else. We're not just a collection of oddballs, you know. We read the Good Book. God's Word, and all that.' She paused, gazing absently at the open Bible. 'It's just that sometimes we have our own interpretations of things.'

Perhaps she had a special interpretation of that red underlined phrase. Craning her neck, Rachel could now see it clearly. It was a passage in Job:

What? Shall we receive good at the hand of God, and shall we not receive evil?

She'd just finished reading it when Ruth reached forward and pushed the book shut. Even the effort of doing that seemed to exhaust her. Her fingers lingered over the Bible for a second, and then she looked squarely at Rachel.

'These are bad times,' she said. 'Sometimes you need the comfort of prayer and the Word just to keep going.'

Rachel nodded, as though she knew what Ruth meant. 'But I don't think you would've said that on Sunday. You looked as high as a kite then. What happened, Ruth?'

'I think you know,' Ruth said. 'Or at least, you have an idea. Otherwise you wouldn't be here, would you?'

Rachel sipped her tea, holding the mug with both hands. The tea was too weak and too sweet, but at least it was hot. 'I suppose we're both thinking about Mr Stands,' she said.

'Both worrying about him,' Ruth added. 'He's the reason you called me, isn't he? Well, I suppose I shocked you, the way I am. But it's all because of him. Since the weekend I've lost four pounds without a diet, and I haven't been sleeping.'

'None of us have been sleeping too well lately.'

'It's *him*,' Ruth went on. 'He's draining me. He's draining all of us here, taking our strength for himself –' She shook her head, suddenly angry. 'When I think how I treated Viv; how I ignored her when she warned me about him! She never trusted him, you know. She told me, but I never listened. All of us, we were all taken in. He blinded us to what he was really doing, and all the time he had us thinking what a blessing he was to have around. I only hope Viv can forgive me after this.'

'I'm sure she realizes it wasn't your fault,' Rachel assured her.

'But it was, in a way. I encouraged him to get

involved. I invited him here as a guest speaker. And he came and talked and gave us hope; he talked about the future, and all the things he could see in the future, and how we only had to want a thing and believe in it to make it happen. He made it sound very simple.' Ruth paused, folding her hands together in front of her. 'I probably don't need to tell you the things we most want here. A future for our town, a livelihood for our children. And so many –' Again she stopped, gnawing her lip, her eyes avoiding Rachel's.

'Go on,' Rachel said, 'it's important.'

'Well, so many people come here because of their loved ones – their dear departed. They need to be comforted. They might've lost a husband or a child, and they don't want to feel they've lost them forever. They want reassurance. They want to believe they'll all be reunited one day. What they want most is to see what happens next, in the next world. In our hearts, I suppose we all want to think it's a good place, and our loved ones are happy there. And we *all* want them back again safe, don't we, unless –' she added with a dry chuckle '– they were more trouble than they were worth while they were alive.'

'Is that what Stands talked about?' Rachel wanted to know. 'The town and the town's future, and the relatives you'd all lost?'

'Not only talked,' Ruth said. 'No, it was much more than that. In the olden days they would've called him a prophet, the way he went on. It was as if – well, he could see into our hearts, he knew what our needs were. Each one of us. He talked about Molly Richardson's husband, Paddy, as if he knew all there was to know about him. He'd died in that terrible flooding at the colliery – what, must be all of ten years ago now. Molly never made much noise about him, kept her thoughts to herself; but now she swears that Paddy's been visiting her every night since . . . since the fête. You see, deep down, Molly always wished he was still with her –'

'And now she has what she wished for.'

'Yes, that's right. She has her husband again. And she's terrified. Why? Because he isn't the same – and how could he be? If you ask me, it's Stands. Stands has brought him back.'

Rachel sat sipping her tea, and now she could barely taste it at all. Suddenly the walls were beginning to feel closer than they should, and Ruth sounded further away. For a moment there was the weirdest impression of patterning on the plain walls; she tried to ignore it. But there was something else too – a faint but sickly taste to the air, which didn't belong. Was it possible Stands could go *that* far? And if so, why would he want to?

'You see,' Ruth continued, 'I think Molly's no different from the rest of us. We hope and wish for things without really thinking of the consequences. Sometimes, when we wish for a thing it's only out of selfishness. It won't do us any good. It's like every dream having its dark side.'

'I can vouch for that,' Rachel began, and was about to go on when Ruth silenced her.

Ruth was frowning towards the coloured streamers which hung in the doorway between the kitchen and chapel. Perhaps she'd heard something, or was waiting to hear something; her eyes seemed to cloud over as she listened. While Ruth watched the streamers, Rachel watched Ruth, hoping that would tell her what was there. She could hear it for herself now, a muffled noise in the next room – a footfall on the soft carpet, perhaps. Then the footsteps, if they were footsteps, halted just outside. Rachel breathed in, someone else breathed out, a shape loomed, a face appeared, the streamers parted.

Ruth smiled. 'Well,' she said to Rachel, 'this is your friend, isn't it?'

Jules came in, still clutching Rachel's note in his hand. He looked pale and slightly shaken and at first his eyes were only on Rachel. She nodded, showing him that everything was fine.

'Some place you have here,' he told Ruth, shivering.

'Oh, the hall and the stairs, you mean. When we took the house over it was all like that. We're still in the process of converting, but it's a big job; it means more money than we have. Why don't you sit down – uh –'

'Jules,' Jules said.

'You look frozen.'

'You look like you just saw a ghost,' Rachel added.

'I saw Dave Brookman,' he said. 'That's the next best thing.'

They traded information while Ruth worked a shuttle-service with the too-weak, too-sweet teas. By five, the light from the slatted window had begun to fade; much too early for summer – but this was no kind of summer at all now. Jules talked about Brookman and Brookman's joyride with Stands, and the face beneath the shadow-man's mask which had driven

Brookman three-parts crazy. Then he listened and heard the story of Paddy Richardson, and again those words, those dreadful words, came back to him: *He could raise the dead if he needed to . . .*

Once or twice he noticed Rachel sniffing the air, frowning. But when he looked at her for an explanation, she could only shake her puzzled head. Something wrong? His hand found·hers under the table. Seeking reassurance, and locking her fingers together with his, Rachel forced their hands upwards on to the table-top, bringing them out to the open.

'You look such a good couple,' Ruth commented, watching them.

Why did that make him feel sad? Usually he would have blushed like a beetroot, but there was no embarrassment now with Rachel; there was only a sadness when they were together, a sadness when she smiled. It had started, he was sure, that night after the fête, down by the waste ground on West End Lane. But now he gave himself a mental kick, trying to forget what she'd said. He mustn't expect things to go wrong, otherwise they would. It was Stands who was doing this to him, making him expect the worst.

Trying to concentrate, he looked at Ruth and wondered how long she'd been talking.

'– is what we call faith,' she was saying. 'When we talk about faith here, we mean that it's all about believing a thing will be done; we don't question it, we just believe in it.'

'That's how it works with Stands,' Rachel said. 'If we believe he can change the town, then he can change the town! If we believe at all, it makes him stronger.'

149

'Exactly,' Ruth said. 'Every wish increases his power. Haven't you noticed how he started off with small miracles when he first came, and how he's been working up to bigger ones ever since? As soon as we started believing in him, he became bigger, stronger, able to do greater and greater things. *That's* why I feel so responsible – because I invited him to our services, I invited him to the fête, I brought him to all those innocent people . . .' She shook her head, angry and frustrated with herself.

'You might as well blame everyone in town,' Jules told her. 'Everyone who ever had a secret wish, and I guess that's most of us. We've all made him strong, because we've all wished for a better town, or wished that things would liven up, or wished for a future or whatever. If that's what made him strong, what can we do about it?'

'How can we stop him?' Rachel asked, looking at Ruth. 'We can't all just pull the plug and stop wanting whatever it is we want.'

'No,' Ruth said, 'obviously we can't do that. But there may be a way of, well, short-circuiting him.'

'What?'

'A way of turning that wish-power against him.' Ruth stared deep into her empty cup, pondering. Then she looked up sharply. 'It seems to me that he spends most of his time around the ones who trust him, the ones he can deceive. Me, for instance. Children, for instance; those children at the infant school. He's especially interested in the children, isn't he?'

'That's what Dave Brookman seemed to think,' Jules said. 'He had the idea that the kids gave Stands his power; because of their wild imaginations.'

'But it's also because they trust him,' Ruth murmured; for a long moment she seemed lost in thought, as though contemplating a very tough cross-word clue, and then she said, 'They really don't doubt him for a minute, do they? They treat him like East-field's own Santa Claus. They think he's good and kind and all things nice, and he never lets them see what he's like . . . underneath.' Now she looked hopefully across the table, first at Rachel, then at Jules. 'Do you think that's because he *needs* their trust? Their faith? Would he have the same kind of power without it? I mean, if the children were shown the kind of monster he is, if they saw for themselves, what do you think would happen then? Perhaps the faith that made him strong could also make him –'

Suddenly she stopped, staring at nothing.

Rachel was sniffing the air, frowning, sniffing again. She looked at Jules, stiffening.

'What's wrong?' he asked. 'You've got yourself a head cold or something?'

She shook her head. 'Don't you smell it? Can't you hear it?'

'Smell what? Hear what?'

Again she shook her head, not quite sure; her touch on his hand weakened as she stared across the kitchen, looking for clues. Then her hand was wrenched completely free as she pointed; pointed towards the two-ring burner. By the time the words had left her lips, Jules could smell and hear it too.

'There!' she cried. 'Gas!'

Chair scraping, Ruth was up and across to the stove like a shot. She stooped and sniffed over one of the rings, and had to whip her head away quickly as if she were dodging a punch.

'Good Lord,' she said, and checked the controls. 'There's nothing turned on! It's flooding out of –'

More chairs scraped, one went over as Rachel, then Jules scrambled to their feet. As they did, the odour and hiss of gas seemed to increase, to fill the room. Ruth went down on her knees, one hand clawing beneath the burner in a quick desperate search for the mains. She found it and turned it off. She gave it one hard final tweak to make sure. It made no difference. The gas whistled in; the stench of it worsened, became overpowering.

'Never mind that,' Jules cried out. Rachel was coughing heavily, both hands fastened over her nose and mouth. 'We haven't got time –'

'I knew it!' Ruth screamed. She was still on her knees, and her eyes were wild. 'I knew it, it's *him*, don't you see? He's making this happen! I know he is –'

'I said *never mind*!'

'He knows we know what he is,' she raced on. 'He knows we're here and what we're saying. He's making this happen, I tell you! He's making this happen to stop us –'

'Come *on*,' Jules insisted, and then his lungs were filling with gas, his eyes were streaming; the gas was numbing his mind. He bolted across the kitchen and had to drag Ruth physically to her feet. She was weighty and hard to budge, and her eyes were lost and far-off. 'Which is the quickest way out?'

'He's trying to destroy our church, he's trying to destroy our good work –'

'Which way?'

She pointed back the way he'd come. In front of the streamers in the doorway, Rachel was bent almost double, the colour gone from her face.

Ruth seemed reluctant to move. Even now, with the kitchen little more than a death-trap, Jules had to force her across the floor to the doorway. She was like the proud, mad captain of a sinking ship who insisted on going down, even with a clean escape staring her in the face.

'All this hard work,' she was crying. 'All the years we've put in . . .'

Save it, he thought, and then yelled at Rachel to move. She was a blurred, choking figure with the kitchen blurring and choking around her; suddenly the walls were higher or lower than they should be, and seemed to be shifting as though they were made of fluid. Jules moved forward, fighting to keep hold of Ruth, and just when he thought Rachel couldn't hear him, or couldn't act, she stumbled out through the streamers to the chapel.

The kitchen was already full of gas; there was nothing to breathe. Ruth was next after Rachel, and as Jules pushed her forward through the doorway, the streamers followed, clinging to her like vines. Ahead there was the chapel, with its altar and its moulded plastic chairs and its three doors giving into the hall, the street, safety. Rachel was already half-way down the aisle, struggling to keep going as she fought for breath. Ruth was just behind her. Jules was battling the streamers in the doorway when the kitchen exploded behind him.

The force of the blast must have flung him several feet, for when he came round he was sprawling in the third row of seats, all arms and legs and merry-go-rounds in his head. His hair had been singed, and some of his clothing, and the smell disgusted him. Rachel was running towards him, a blank shape surrounded by yellow light, her voice choked by tears as much as by fumes.

'Jules? Oh thank God you're all right!' She huddled around him, holding him gently, easing him up. Behind her, the kitchen doorway was the mouth of a bright-burning furnace. 'Can you walk?' she was saying. 'Can you use your legs?'

Now it was the smell of scorching and smoke which filled the house. Sections of table, chair, sink unit, stove had been thrown in chunks through to the chapel; each was a separate spreading fire, hungry for something to burn. The air was turning black; moulded chairs re-moulded themselves, melting, forming new shapes.

Where was Ruth? Jules looked madly about, trying to pick her out through the smoke. Then he could see her working at one of the doors, forcing the handle, hammering the door with her shoulder.

They moved along the row of seats, stumbling over themselves, kicking the seats out of the way. The heat was unbearable now, but in a second or two they'd be free of it. So why was Ruth faltering at the door? Why had she turned away from it instead of prizing it open? As they neared the end of the row, Rachel called, 'You're at the wrong one! That one's locked! Go to the next one down –'

But Ruth's face, when she turned towards them, was a hot, reddened picture of defeat. 'But I've tried them *all*! They're all like this!'

'They can't be,' Jules said, more to himself than the others, and then he was fumbling from the row of seats, blinded by smoke, tearing at the first door, the second door, the third. None of them budged, even when he thrust his shoulder hard against the wood; they were all stubbornly sealed. How could they be, when he and Rachel had come in this way? He turned and fell against the wall, trying to think, trying to hold his breath against the smoke. He looked quickly across the room, past Rachel, past Ruth, to the roller-blinded windows at the end. Perhaps they could get through there, perhaps they could use the seats to smash through . . . But even as he looked, another wall appeared out of nowhere, a blistering wall of flame between him and the windows, sealing the windows off.

For a second he was on the verge of a blackout; he felt himself sliding uselessly down the wall, losing himself. Then there were firm hands grabbing him, shaking him. Rachel was with him, barely able to support herself, let alone him.

'Don't go yet,' she was telling him. 'Don't give up on us yet –'

'Stranded,' he heard himself say, and the words hardly made sense anymore; they were noises without meaning. 'We're stranded, we don't have anywhere to go.'

'Don't . . . give . . . up . . .'

They were hemmed between two of the doors, surrounded by fire. There was no way forward to the windows, no way back. The chairs were down to the metal frames, and plastic slimed off them like mud; and the walls were alive with bright-burning wallpaper, charred black scraps of it filling the air. As Jules felt his eyes closing on the scene, Rachel collapsed against him, holding tight.

'This isn't it,' she whispered, perhaps to herself. 'This isn't the Dark Place, it can't be over yet . . .' She tailed off, her words so quiet he couldn't hear them, and again he could feel himself drifting, away from the blazing room, away from the pain of the burns he'd received, towards a quiet and comfortable place, a nice cool place where he could rest. He drifted and enjoyed it, enjoyed the feeling, until he heard Rachel calling.

'Wake, up, Jules, and look! Wake up!'

He opened his eyes and he was back in the fire again. Somewhere in front of him, Ruth was down on her knees. Her head was bowed but her eyes were focused on something across the room. For a moment he thought she was praying, but no one prayed like that – not with their mouths agape, not with their features twisted in terror. When he glanced at Rachel, he found the very same terror – open-mouthed, eyes widened and disbelieving. Whatever Ruth was seeing, she was seeing. He followed the line of her gaze, to a place beyond the shrivelling seats, to the altar itself;

and then he could see what they saw. He could see it but couldn't believe it.

Stands was there. Across the room, at the altar, raised on the makeshift platform, Stands was there. He stood at the lectern, surrounded by fire, yet the flames didn't touch him. Nothing touched him, not even the thick palls of smoke which rose from the altar.

Jules could feel every last glimmer of hope drain out of him. It was as if the shadow-man had risen from the fire itself, as if he were *part* of the fire. He was wearing his mask – not the crumbling, rotting mask Brookman had seen, but the same darkly grinning Mr Nice Guy mask that had suckered too many people already. Still grinning, he began to lift both his hands to the air – a conjurer, Jules thought, about to start his act. His eyes were poisonous, piercing Jules even through the smoke, across the grey clouded space. Behind him, the wall-hung tapestry had become a blazing backdrop for his performance.

So much for your faith, Jules thought bitterly, looking at Ruth. She was still on her knees and visibly shaking, out of control. How's your faith going to help us now? But it wasn't her fault, it wasn't anyone's fault. Only the shadow-man's, only his.

Beside him, Rachel made a deep, low, groaning sound . . .

At the altar, Stands had reached up and plucked a spray of flowers from the flames, from the smoke. Black smoke, yellow flames, red roses. For a second he smiled approvingly at the trick, and then –

Encore!

He thrust the flowers up, high over his head, hurling

them at the ceiling. At once the red roses were no longer red roses but separate exploding fireballs; yellow and orange and blue liquid fire covered the ceiling, swallowed it up. Droplets of flame fell, landed, destroyed.

'And are you going to believe in me now?' Stands mocked. He was far away, little more than a dark blur which bent and shimmered in the heat. He raised a hand, extended a finger. 'And are you going to believe in me now?'

I always believed in you, Jules thought, *I just didn't want you, that's all –*

A white streak of lightning flashed from the shadow-man's finger; a vast angry pillar of fire reared up where it landed. The heat it give out seemed incredible, impossible; even the air itself was burning now. Jules could feel himself slipping again, paralysed by heat and by smoke. Sirens wailed somewhere deep in his mind. Sirens that grew louder as he grew weaker. Then there was only the illusion – and it must have been an illusion – of Stands warping and twisting in the heat at the altar, and changing shape, and changing colour, until he was white and yellow and blue and orange and nothing more than another furious tongue of fire.

Jules blinked, trying to rid himself of the vision, but there was no shadow-man to see. There was only the burning room with its walls of fire and ceilings of fire, and the three of them snookered against the door, all gradually sliding to the floor as if melting. The end, he thought stupidly. The end of the game. Even the sirens had stopped in his head; perhaps they'd surrendered and given up too. Weakly, with no strength left in him, he stretched out a hand to Rachel – at least she was there, the one he cared about, the one who mattered. Seeing him, Rachel returned his gesture and put out her hand. Their fingers met across the boiling panels of the door, their hands linked together. As they touched, the door split apart down the middle.

The shock of it pulled them apart at once. Splinters and chips of wood rained inwards, adding fuel to the fire. Just for a second Jules looked at Rachel, Rachel at Jules, their mouths agog. Then a second impact shook the door, cracking, splintering; the narrow split widened. There was the briefest glint of something sharp, cold, metallic and then – another blow, another. A split, a gash, a hole opened up. An axe-head gleamed.

It may have only been seconds before the rest of the door fell inwards, but it seemed much longer than that. Before Jules could truly register – truly believe – what was happening, there were man-sized shapes in the wide-open doorway; shapes in bright-buttoned uniforms and hard, jutting helmets, their faces obscene and misshapen. Then he realized their faces were masks. Some wielded axes, some carried long, brassy nozzles like weird staring musket-barrels; some stepped aside when they saw him. At first he didn't move, because he couldn't. He felt unable to drag himself even as far as the doorway. One pair of heavy gloved hands grabbed him, threw him. He was half falling, half stumbling out to the hallway when someone yelled, 'Out! *Out!* Just get a bloody move on and don't look back!'

He checked briefly over his shoulder just in time to see Rachel come tumbling after him, her legs barely holding her, and then Ruth Parsons, who wasn't moving at all but was sagging in the arms of one of the shapes.

'Out!' Rachel called, echoing the order.

Then they were away from the doorway, away from the furnace, and negotiating the tumbledown hall, past the other locked doors, past the paint-peeling walls, past the twin heaps of seats at the foot of the stairs; then on through the main door to the marvellous, wonderful sights of cold white snow, the bright red telephone box across the street, the two bright red fire engines parked in front of the house – and, at the bottom of the steps, the glowing, disbelieving face of Steve Harper.

'I'm sorry I'm late,' he said.

20

They all converged on Jules's room – Jules and Rachel, who both sat cross-legged on the bed, and Steve Harper, who didn't. Steve was down on all fours as though worshipping the rack of hi-fi components that towered above him, but in fact he was going through Jules's record collection, and pausing thoughtfully over each sleeve in turn, the way you always did with other people's. He wrinkled his nose at John Cooper Clarke and pushed him back in the pile, ignored Frankie altogether, then looked up sharply.

'Hey Jules, I didn't know you had a whole set of Comsat Angels LPs.'

'Neither did I,' Jules told him.

'Or all these U2s or this Steely Dan.'

'Me neither.'

'I guess Santa came a-calling early this year.'

'I guess.'

Steve shook his head, picked out a record called *Sleep No More*, then stood and puzzled out how to get the hi-fi working. It was Steve who'd telephoned the fire brigade, arriving on Moxon Street just as the blaze took hold in the chapel; the houselights he could see from the bottom of the road had turned out not to be houselights after all. When the doors in the hall had refused to open he'd hell-for-leathered it across to the phone box; just, as it happened, in time.

Remarkably, no one had been seriously burned. Even more remarkably, Rachel had come out of it right as rain; only her clothing had scorched and, once her lungs had begun to clear and her senses had restored themselves, the rest of her seemed to be fine. Jules had got away with a reddened boiled-lobsterish look to his face and hands, nothing worse than a mild case of sunburn. There was really only Ruth Parsons who'd been anywhere near seriously hurt; the fumes had put her out of the game, and now the word was she was recuperating back where she started, and where *all* of this started for her – in a hospital bed.

For the last hour and a half, Jules's mother had been ferrying in the coffee and sandwiches, and so far she'd been amazingly quiet, passing a few pleasantries with Rachel and Steve, but saying little or nothing about what had happened. Jules knew exactly what that meant. It meant she was appalled, horrified, on the verge of despair and had plenty to say, but was saving it. She'd sealed herself up like a jar; she'd lost a daughter and almost gained a corpse for a son – not at all the way things were supposed to work out. Even his dad looked tortured now, with nothing to say. All he'd said, or been able to say as they came into the house was, 'Thank goodness . . . thank goodness you're safe.' But his eyes had been full of questions, far more questions than Jules could ever hope to answer. Later, Jules thought, later, the talk would start. Perhaps that was when he would have to tell them, finally tell them, all he knew about Stands.

Steve had cracked the hi-fi code and was adjusting the volume while the Comsats chimed through the first of their tracks.

'So what about the library?' Jules asked.

'Nothing,' Steve said. 'Just a big zero. No back issues of the local press, apart from the last three months, and the record books seem to cover everything that's mundane and useless and come to a halt around 1935.'

'And Ruth wasn't so much help either,' Jules said. 'I'd thought she might be hand-in-hand with the creep but she's as lost as the rest of us. So we're back where we started. We're going round in circles.'

'But it isn't as bad as you make it sound,' Rachel said. 'I'm sure there's something in what Ruth was saying; about short-circuiting his power, about turning the children against him. I'm sure that's why Stands tried to stop her, when she started talking about that. As soon as she did, that's when it happened, isn't it? Well,' she enthused, glancing from Jules to Steve and back again, 'don't you think she was right? The kids, the ones with the crazy imaginations, they're the key. If what she was saying is right, if the wish-power can be used against him ... we might have found his weakness.' She stopped and waited for a response, watching the others closely. 'Well?' she prompted.

'Well, you could be right,' Jules offered. 'There could be a weakness. But we haven't found Laurie. We're no nearer to that than we ever were.'

'Defeatist.'

'That's me.'

'Well don't be,' Steve Harper said. 'And don't be so

quick to admit it, either. We haven't even started yet, and here's you all set and ready to give up.'

'I'm sorry. You're right. As always.'

'As always,' Steve agreed. He was looking around for something other than the carpet to sit on, finally selecting a chair which stood in front of the window. One of Jules's jackets had been draped over the back of it. He took hold of the chair and began, idly, to drag it across to the bedside.

Watching him, Jules couldn't help thinking again of that morning at the hospital, visiting Gran, and all the white faces and shocks of white hair; all those old folks waving and chirping like children. Suddenly he could almost imagine the town in the wake of the shadow-man: the old folks would be young folks, six-year-olds would be sixteen-year-olds, those who wanted it would have their promotions and raises and flit from small red-brown houses to enormous white ones with vast green lawns and long, sweeping driveways. No one right now seemed satisfied just to be who and what they were; but Stands could change all of that. He could put the smiles back on their faces, alter their lives, turn the whole damn lot of them into perfect, grinning zombies. If that was what they wanted.

'What's that?' Steve Harper was wondering.

As he'd been nearing the bedside, something had tumbled from the jacket slung over the chair-back; it hit the floor with a very slight thump. It was only last week's *Courier*, the one Rachel had left in the greasy café and which Jules had afterwards stuffed in his pocket.

'Drop it over there in the waste bin,' Jules said, pointing.

Steve nodded as he picked up the newspaper and sat down with it. 'In a minute.' Settling on the chair, he turned one page, another page, scanning the columns as you might scan the columns in the dentist's waiting room, your mind on more important things.

Jules lolled tiredly on the bed, rocking ever so slightly back and forth to the Comsat beat, though out of keep with it. The song was a thing called 'Be Brave'.

Rachel folded herself into a half sitting, half lying position, one shoeless foot dangling over the edge, keeping time.

The music exploded:

> *Out of the dark, into the light*
> *Looking for a way round it*
> *When it calls, you won't hear*
> *You will shout and will drown it out –*

Suddenly Steve Harper's face lit up. He sat bolt upright, very nearly jumping out of his seat. He slammed one fist into the newspaper he held with such force, Jules was sure it would disintegrate in his hands.

'See this? See this?' he shouted, and thrust the week-old *Courier* at Jules. 'Is this what we've been looking for?' Then he managed to calm himself and spoke more softly. 'I think it's what we've been looking for.'

Rachel was pulling herself over to see, while Jules spread the newspaper flat out on the bed. At first he saw only news which had been and gone: FÊTE TO BE HELD THIS SUNDAY – HEATWAVE FORECAST. And then a small headline which seemed all too close for comfort: CAR STOLEN – but that turned out to be a blue Citroen on Beech Street, nothing to do with Vauxhalls or, for that matter, with Mercs.

Finally his finger came to rest on a story about half-way down the page, and he read it twice over, hardly daring to breathe:

MEMORIAL SET FOR 29TH

A memorial service is to be held for the victims of the worst mining disaster in Eastfield's history. The service, which takes place on the 29th of this month, will pay tribute to the fourteen miners who lost their lives during underground flooding at Eastfield colliery ten years ago.

Relatives of the deceased have asked for a public rather than private service for what some have referred to as the 'anniversary memorial'. The service will be held at Eastfield All Saints church, and among those expected to attend are . . .

When Jules looked up from the newspaper at last, the air in the room felt electric. He could sense it along his arms and legs, at the back of his neck, a hum and a tingle of nerve-ends. Whatever it was, he could see it written across Steve's face and across Rachel's; the same fearful wonder. Was this it? Was this what Stands had been baiting him with? And the damn thing sitting there in his pocket all along?

'Are you thinking what I'm thinking?' Steve asked.

'I'm not sure. What *are* you thinking?'

'The colliery,' Steve said. 'Not the church but the mine. He's underground. Somewhere down there, at the mine.'

'The Dark Place,' Rachel added, almost in a whisper, speaking so softly that neither Steve nor Jules heard her; it must have been meant for herself.

PART THREE

The Wishbringer

—— *21* ——

There were two possible approaches you could make to the pit yard. One, which the motorists once took, ran flatly and narrowly from the top of Station Lane to the main gates, between boarded-up council houses and disused fields where the trains cut their way across country. During the miners' strike the road had been covered with oil and with nails, and patrolled by pickets. If you walked or drove that way now you'd still see the up-ended shell of a burnt-out car at the roadside, in a ditch in front of the fields; you'd see all the scars of the battles there.

The other approach was quicker, but all uphill. A sprawling footpath wobbled up across a field behind the Church Hill estate; the field was used as a local dump, and today the shapes of old prams on their sides and cartons of newspaper rose out of the snow, and the footpath had disappeared. As they walked up the field, Jules and Rachel and Steve Harper saw the mineworkings grow larger ahead of them, and when they looked back they saw the town growing smaller. The mine was surrounded by squat, white hills, which underneath the snow were slack-heaps. But if the snow thawed now, this instant, you'd still believe they were hills; a few years ago they'd sown the slack-heaps with grass seeds, so that pleasant green mounds would look down on the town instead of depressing grey ones.

It made little difference to Jules, though. He grew more uncomfortable as the mine became larger, closer. The mineworkings were still grey, and today seemed greyer than ever before against the miles of whiteness around them. Stands was up there. Stands, together with Laurie, waiting for tomorrow's anniversary memorial for the miners. If they didn't find him here, now, today, they were finished, there'd be nothing they could do. They were almost at the gates when Steve Harper stopped, and gave Jules a nudge.

'Listen,' Steve told him.

'Look,' said Rachel.

They listened and looked and kept very quiet, the three of them very small in the large white field with the sound of the wind blowing across it, the wind blowing cold in their faces. But there was something else in the wind, not hot, not cold, not even the sound of their clothes and hair thrashing. It was the grumble and churn of machinery, a wheeze of metal on metal that set Jules thinking of late night distant trains, slow local trains slowing as they crawled to the station platform. Up high above them, high above the colliery, a big wheel turned. It turned very slowly but turned all the same.

'Look,' Rachel said. 'It's that — what do you call those things?'

'They call it the headgear,' Steve told her. 'It carries the cage — a kind of lift they use to go down to the seams. My dad took me down in it once, before they made him redundant.'

'Before they made everyone redundant,' Jules said.

'I know that sound,' Rachel said.

'From where?' Steve asked.

She looked at Jules, her cheeks rose-red in the cold. 'This is the place, isn't it?'

'If it isn't,' Jules said, 'then who the hell's up there working it?'

'We're close,' Steve said, and held up a finger and thumb. 'We're *that* close. Can't you feel it?'

Jules gave a nod. He could. That was the thing that gnawed inside him, bunching the nerves of his stomach. There was only one thing worse than the prospect of not finding Stands, and that was the prospect of finding him. *But what will we do if he is there?* he thought. *What can we do? We didn't come this far to run, that's all; we didn't come to back down.*

The rear gates were wrought-iron bars which rose up to devilish points, and the two large sections were padlocked together. The chain which held them had just enough slack to let them squeeze through; given a push, the gates parted eight or ten inches. With Rachel in front and Steve last, they wriggled in through the gap to the pit yard.

The yard was as cluttered as a scrap merchant's. Broken and rusted sections of old burnt-out rattletraps stood in snow-blown piles; huge coils of rope lay waiting like sleeping snakes; in one corner a tub-like paddy-car lolled on its side, wheels unmoving, and in another there were long strips of track leading nowhere. Most of the buildings here were squat, grey lumps with hints of red brick beneath the grime, and the thin layer of snow underfoot was stained by coal dust.

Overhead, the big wheel turned, groaning, and for a moment Jules felt he'd wandered into a ghost-haunted funfair.

'Is the lift coming up or going down?' Rachel wondered.

Steve watched the headgear, and shrugged.

'Who do you think's riding in it?' she asked.

'I'd rather not think,' Steve told her. 'I guess we'll find out soon enough.'

'So what now?' Jules said. 'Do we find a way down?'

'We'll take a look around first,' Steve decided. 'We really need masks and lamps. There'll be gas and probably water down there. They'll have shut off all the pumps and ventilation.'

'Do your folks know we're here?' Rachel asked Jules as Steve led the way across the yard, past a flat-roofed sawmill with small dark windows.

Jules shook his head. 'I told them everything else, but I didn't tell them about this. I mean, we couldn't be sure that this was the place –'

'But now we can be sure.'

'Yes.'

'Do you think we should bring the cops up here before we go any further?'

'Do you think it'll make any difference?'

Rachel shrugged. 'There's nothing they can do. There's nothing anyone can do to change things.' Suddenly she became tense and anxious, and reached for his hand. 'I think this is it, Jules. It's where the dreams have been bringing me. It's where they end.'

He looked away from her, as if that would stop his

174

thoughts. If something went wrong today, if they were trapped by gas or by water or a fall in one of the seams, no one would know where to find them. It wouldn't only be the end of Rachel's dream but the end, full stop. But he was being defeatist again; the mine had been closed for only a matter of weeks — even with everything shut off it ought to be safe. Steve had told him that, and Steve usually knew what he was talking about. He was worrying for himself again, as always, when really it was Laurie he ought to be worried about, down there in the dark with only the shadow-man for company; briefly, he hated himself for being so selfish.

Steve was waiting in the doorway of one of the flat, bland buildings.

'Anyone for a shower?' he asked, as they followed him in.

The shower room was white-tiled from ceiling to floor, and stank faintly of stale water. Shower heads in lines poked down from the ceiling, overhanging cubicles without doors, and one of the shower heads dripped with a regular pat, echoing off the tiles. They walked through, wet shoes skidding, and into a cramped adjoining room full of lockers.

Most of the lockers had busted locks, or none at all. Steve began slapping them open, dumping their contents on the floor. A couple of pairs of steel-toed boots, a plastic comb, several pairs of faded blue overalls that coughed up black dust as they landed.

'Grab,' Steve said, and tossed a white safety helmet at Jules, and one at Rachel. When Rachel tried hers for size she giggled, for the contraption almost covered her eyes.

'Cute,' Steve told her. 'You look like a sheepdog peeking through its fringe.'

'Thanks,' Rachel said, and picked up and tried another, which made no difference at all.

In one locker Steve found a khaki-coloured rucksack and emptied that too; a thermos flask tumbled out, as did something greyish green that might have passed for a sandwich, once.

Satisfied, Steve threw the rucksack over his shoulder and gave it a tap. 'Something to put our kit in, if we find any,' he explained. 'You want boots or boiler suits?'

Jules shook his head.

'I can't see me in those,' Rachel said.

'Then try these knee-pads,' Steve said, and threw them. 'If we've any crawling to do you'll be glad of them.'

'What else do we need?' Jules asked.

Steve considered. 'They might have cleared everything else out. If we're lucky there might be some lamps to go with the helmets. Then we'll want battery belts and dust-masks, and I think they usually carried gas masks for emergencies. We'll need tools – hammers, picks, whatever – I think I can get those in the blacksmith's workshop. If all that gear's gone, though,' he added, 'we'll have to forget it. It wouldn't be safe.'

'It won't be safe as it is,' Jules said.

After the locker room, they came to a wall of pigeon-holes stuffed with black rubbery dust-masks. Steve stopped to sort through them, throwing some down, setting aside the newest and cleanest.

'The strap goes over your head like this,' he demonstrated, slinging one on, 'and the rest fits over your nose and mouth.' He removed the mask, dropped it in the rucksack, dropped in another two after it.

Seconds later they were back to the dull, pale sky and the moans of machines. While Steve ran hunting for the blacksmith's, Jules stood with Rachel outside a wooden prefabricated hut with broken windows and Nice Cool Ice Cool Milk stickers on the walls. There was nothing inside but dust and rubble; perhaps the hut had once been a canteen. As he looked at Rachel, Jules found that same bitter sadness again sagging deadweight inside his chest. He wished it would leave him alone; he couldn't deal with it now.

'I've been thinking,' he said. 'Maybe it'd be better if you stayed here while we went down. It's safer.'

'Uh-oh,' she smiled. 'You're not going to give me that fairer-sex crap or that this-is-men's-work crap are you? I can handle it, Jules, honest I can.'

'It's just that up here it's safer. I don't want you where Stands can get at you.'

'Well, it's a bit late for that. We've all been got at.' She looked past him, across the pit yard, and her eyes had that far-away look again, as if she saw something he couldn't. 'And I *have* to go, don't you see? I don't think I have a choice, really, at all.'

He let it ride, but only because the sounds had stopped him. The ground beneath their feet was beginning to tremble, and tremble as if it were haunted. Perhaps the sound of machinery had been in his dreams too, for he was sure he knew it. Incredibly, the old pit seemed to be ticking over again, so that now he could feel it within himself, in his cold arms and legs, in his bones; a gathering of life in old machines. He listened, and the ground shuddered.

Was any of that possible? Towards the end, before they finally closed the mine, colliers had worked their last weeks here in a long, drawn-out salvage operation, removing all the underground equipment and bringing it out to the surface. There should be nothing down there now but empty blackness, a maze of tunnels. Then he remembered Stands, that day in the fortune-tent, and those words which should have meant good news but instead meant anything but:

By the time I'm finished here, people are gonna be in work again . . . They're gonna be living good lives . . .

Was this how he planned to put the town back on its feet; by restoring the mine, by making it profitable again? After all, wasn't that the one thing everyone in town had been wishing for? Of course it was. Those fed-up faces you'd see in the street would perk up as if by magic at the first whiff of work. Happiness here was a million tons of coal a year, because that had been the town's future and, without that, Eastfield was nothing more than a ghost town.

High across the yard the headgear had stopped turning. There was a quick flurry of movement on the ground below, and Jules saw that it was Steve Harper, small in the distance, waving them over.

'What does that mean?' Rachel asked once they'd trudged across the snowbound yard. She was indicating the headgear.

'It might mean the cage is all the way down,' Steve told her, staggering slightly with the weighted ruck-sack, which now bulged and clanked full of tools.

'Either that, or it's all the way up and waiting to take us down.'

'God help us,' Jules whimpered. 'You think he *wants* us down there? You think he's actually inviting us?'

'Could be. He's in control, isn't he?'

'Well, I only hope you polished your crucifix,' Jules said. But that was without humour, and no one laughed. Even Steve Harper was beginning to look past laughter now.

There was one last call to make. In a cabin near the shaft side, there were helmet-lamps and battery belts and one or two brass miner's oil lamps, of the sort you'd find hanging in traditional pubs or decorating local mantelshelves. Most of the gear was defective, but enough of it worked. The oil lamps, Steve explained, were used to check for gas; you lighted the lamp before you went down, and if its brightness dimmed or went out you reached for the safety masks, and quick.

When they had what they needed they went out from the lamp cabin and into the piercing wind and the rumble of underground workings, and stood in front of the shaft-side building, a fat, grey Lego block beneath the big wheel. The entrance, a large, dark doorway without a door, gave on to a set of concrete steps which were shadowed in secrecy. The mouth of the monster, Jules couldn't help thinking.

'Are you sure –' he began.

'Ssshhh,' Rachel hissed, then ruffled his hair. 'I'm going. Just try and stop me.'

179

The steps were icy, and crackled and shifted under-foot; the walls were a sickly lime-green which echoed their steps, echoed the jangle of tools. At the top of the flight they turned into a tiled, almost tunnel-like corridor, and suddenly they were moving faster than they wanted, stumbling forward in the half-light. The air was far colder here, colder even than the wind outdoors, and seemed to be pulling them on, drawing them in. The brightness of day was behind them, gone, and ahead there was only –

'Why are we being pulled?' Jules gasped. He was almost into a jog now, with no control of his legs.

'Suction, I think,' Steve said. 'It's from the shaft, it works like a vacuum.'

Jules stumbled on. But there was more to it than that, wasn't there? The shaft might be dragging them along, but in his way, so was Stands. Like flies to a spider's web, Jules thought, shuddering. Like lambs to the . . .

But he had to stop thinking that way. You couldn't afford to think, you just had to go and do; you mustn't imagine, you mustn't imagine the worst, for that'd be playing into the shadow-man's hands; you had to stay calm and think of Laurie, think only of her.

The tunnel sucked him onward. Half-way along it, the cage was waiting. It stood suspended by two heavy ropes, which reached upwards through a gap in the roof to the headgear's pulleys, and stood open-jawed, yawning. Its huge, up-sliding door was constructed in cross-hatched metal, and was already thrown wide open. The grey metal walls inside looked solid but blank. So Steve had guessed right; the cage had been travel-ling up, not down, and it wanted to take them with it.

They stood at the entrance looking in, just as you might stand over and watch a waterfall, seeing it clearly, not really wanting to step in and join it. High above them, the faintest creak of pulleys.

'How do we work this thing?' Jules said to Steve.

'There's a control room somewhere,' Steve told him. 'They used to have a man in there, operating. But I wouldn't know how to. Maybe there's a button or something inside,' he added, and took a very small step forward.

After a moment's thought he took another. Then he stepped in.

Before Jules could stop her, Rachel had followed Steve inside the cage. She put on her too-large helmet and peered at him from under the peak.

'You can come too, if you like,' she told him.

'For the last time of asking –' Jules started, but she shook her helmeted head slowly, deliberately, and he quickly fell silent. Like Jules, she'd been drawn to this place, she'd been pulled towards it, just as the air pressure had pulled them; and now she wanted to know why. There was no use arguing.

'There're no controls here,' Steve was complaining, studying the vacant grey walls. 'I'm not sure what we do now.' Frustrated, he struck the metal casing with a fist. It grumbled like a heavy gong.

That was the moment the cage-door dropped. Steve must have seen it or sensed it coming, since he rolled away from the wall on that side in an instant. The door slammed down like a guillotine; the impact rocked the cage, and the one long deafening crash of metal sang forever. Then the door was closed, sealing them in, and there was only the after-echo of noise way back in the tunnel, or perhaps way below them in the shaft. High up above the roof, the headgear groaned.

'I think we're on our way,' someone said, and Jules couldn't be sure who'd spoken. Perhaps it was him.

All at once he could feel the moisture leave his mouth, his tongue becoming dry as paper. His heart was pounding, but he couldn't hear it, because of the churn of machinery, the wheeze of pulleys.

The half-lit world was slipping from sight above him, and cold clammy darkness enclosed the cage. It had happened too quickly; the sudden rush of blackness almost panicked him into a cry. He began grappling for the on-switch of his headlamp, and found it and flicked it; and for some reason remembered the ragged banner from the fortune-tent rending itself on a rail in the storm – *Let there be light*, it had said.

And then there *was* light in the dark, the light from his headlamp, and from the brass gas-detecting oil lamp which Steve was lighting. But still not enough light, he thought.

They were going down to the Dark Place. And suddenly he knew something he hadn't known before, something he wouldn't have believed this morning, or an hour ago, or five minutes ago.

They weren't going to have to find Stands after all. The hunt was over. The search had finished before it could begin. Stands was bringing them to himself.

—— 22 ——

'Hear that?' Rachel said.

'Hear what?'

Silence.

As the cage descended, as the darkness rushed up and the coal seam arrived with a jolt, Jules could begin to hear it too. The headgear whined faintly miles above them, ropes tickered under the strain, but other than that, silence ruled. The rumble and throb of under-ground machinery had stopped.

'Even the bloody machines are expecting us,' Jules murmured.

They came out into the dark, clammy shaft, where the air seemed heavier than sackcloth. Already, before they'd begun to move, Jules could taste the dust in his mouth, could feel it clogging his nostrils. Rachel was gagging and trying to fix on her face-mask. When he looked towards her the white of her headlamp blinded him, reminded him of something – a dream perhaps, of clamouring one-eyed creatures on a ghost-ride, of Cyclops-eyed things crawling towards him. Now he could see, he could understand: their eyes hadn't been eyes of course, but blasts of harsh torchlight like those on their helmets. Had he dreamt it or seen it somewhere, perhaps in a film? He couldn't remember, but maybe it didn't matter. Rachel had moved her head again, and the illusion was gone.

'Where do we go from here?' he asked, his words full of grit.

'Down here,' Steve suggested; they set off. They were in a kind of roadway network which connected one seam with another. Ahead there was only gloom in the narrow tunnel, and perhaps an L-shaped turning which might be another roadway. In the weird wash of light from their lamps, silver droplets of water fell and landed with a steady, slime-sounding patter. The dust rose in clouds as they walked. Was this what they'd wished for, all those donkey-jacketed dole-holers in Eastfield? Did they really want to come back to *this*?

He wondered.

Perhaps it was true; perhaps it *was* all they wanted. After all, it was their livelihood, it was all they knew. But none of them could know, could they, how bad it might be if their wishes came true. That's how easy it was to be fooled, once your heart was set on a thing.

At the end of the roadway they turned into another. Here there were creaks and groans from the low beams and arch-girders supporting the roof, and they had to stoop as they moved. Thickening dust formed a screen in front of them, throwing the lamplight back in their faces. Drops of water drummed on their helmets, and at some point Rachel made a sound of digust as one of the drops found the nape of her neck. It was impossible to see more than six or eight feet ahead now, and maybe the shadow-man was only a few feet further on, hiding where he couldn't be seen, silently mocking them.

'Why doesn't he show himself?' Jules whispered; his whisper came back a hundred times off the walls. 'He practically invited us here, didn't he? So why doesn't he show himself?'

But there was no answer to that, and neither Steve nor Rachel tried to give one. They walked for a few more seconds, just until Jules felt something collide with his foot. It was hard and metallic, and at once he knew he should have been wearing steel-capped boots. It took a few seconds before the pain speared his leg, ran like a bolt of electricity from toe up to knee. He cursed, stumbled, grabbed at the pain, but the pain was in too many places at once. He stood cursing, wobbling on one leg like a foul-mouthed flamingo.

'See here?' Steve Harper was saying.

They all looked down. Their lights washed over the standard-gauge rail line; it was the very beginning or the very end of the track, depending on which way you faced.

'And see there?' Steve said. He was gesturing now along the roadway, where a solid, dark mass blocked the way. 'Looks like we have ourselves some transport.'

He started towards it, with Jules limping after. The pain had steadied itself into a dull, aching throb. Rachel was with him.

'Would you like me to be your crutch?' she said.

'I'll live,' he told her.

'That's the spirit. Think of England. Think of East-field.'

They approached the rear sections of the mini-train. There were coal-filled tubs at intervals, and cars which had bench-like seats for the colliers to use. Very short, stooping colliers they must have been, who might easily have lost their heads to the roof.

'It's a rope-haulage system,' Steve said. 'No engine, no driver. There's a signal box somewhere along the track, and the whole thing used to be operated from a control room upstairs. You pressed the go–button and *whoosh*, off you went. Well, we can't do that now. There's no one to –'

'But we don't need to do *anything*,' Rachel said keenly.

They looked at her, though her face was lost behind the Cyclops–eye of light.

'It's my guess we only have to sit in it,' she went on. '*He*'ll do the rest. We didn't need anyone to work the cage, did we?'

Somewhere an arch-girder creaked, black water dripped.

'Well, he brought us this far, didn't he?' she insisted.

But Steve was already heaving his rucksack into the car and climbing in after it. When Jules had got in with Rachel, they sat there for a moment, quite still, waiting, nothing happening, feeling foolish; a cough, a shuffle, the sting of grit in their eyes.

Perhaps we are being stupid, Jules thought. Rachel was removing her dust-mask and wiping her mouth. *Perhaps we're fooling ourselves, the way Laurie got fooled and Ruth Parsons got fooled . . . Maybe he's just playing cat-and-mouse with us before he finishes the job good and proper; and what do you think he brought you down here for anyway? Tiffin?*

'Uh-oh,' Steve groaned suddenly, and when Jules

looked he thought he could see the oil lamp flickering, growing dimmer. It couldn't be an illusion, for Steve was staring at it between his hands, staring as though his life depended on its yellow glow.

'Perhaps we ought to get out of –' Jules started, then stopped, as the oil lamp flickered and died, and Steve's headlamp went out, and Jules's next, and Rachel's.

They sat, scarcely breathing, in darkness. It had come as sure and as quick as death; a darkness as large and complete as the darkness inside Ruth Parsons' fortune-tent. It fell over everything, making him blind. Rachel was gone; Steve was gone; suddenly the dripping sounds, the groans of beams were far too close for comfort, and at first that was all there was – a dripping and groaning, a dripping and groaning echo.

But there was something more. Beside him, Rachel was listening, rigid, as first the sigh, then the wheeze, then the clatter of noise started up. This time the noise wasn't ahead of them, and neither was it above or below them.

'We're moving,' Rachel said.

And they were. It was the clatter of wheels and wagons on tracks he'd heard; the sound of it smothered him like the dust he couldn't see, and now it was hauling them forward, through blackness and under low-hanging beams, between walls that were narrower than the span of his arms. Somewhere further on, Stands would be waiting. Waiting and grinning. Just around the next corner, or the next one, or the one after that.

Years ago, he'd cried out loud on the Scarborough ghost-train while green and luminous skeletons and demons with death's-head faces swelled from the walls; and one had been close enough to brush his cheek, and he'd cried out again, with pleasure. There was no pleasure now, though — only the cold rushing air, the heavy dust. But what did he hear, off there in the dark? Even above the noise of the cars on the tracks, he heard it.

One long, shrill cry had gone up in the tunnel. Almost an Indian war-whoop, he thought, like the ones he'd made those times on the ghost-train. But it wasn't his and it wasn't Rachel's or Steve's, for sure. It rolled around the walls like a boat in a storm, rising, falling. In fact it was nearer a laugh than a cry — and yes, that was it, the mad, laughing whoop was the shadow-man's, no other sound like it, no question.

There were pin-pricks of light up ahead now. They seemed to come alive one by one, like the distant lights of a town. And the train was slowing. Was the shadow-man's howl behind or ahead of them? It came from all places at once, off the roofing, off the walls, the unworldly call of some prehistoric beast. There was nothing human about it, Jules thought, and since when did even a beast sound like that?

Steve was fumbling blind through the rucksack and taking something out. Clutching at Jules's hand, Rachel was muttering incoherently, and he couldn't make out her words for the noise. He puzzled over the lights ahead, watching them grow and sweep closer. What was it Rachel was saying? What was she aiming her finger at? When she finally stopped pointing and slapped her free hand over her mouth to stifle a cry, Jules could see what she'd seen. The lights were not where he'd thought, some short distance along the tunnel in front of them. The lights were on the train.

They were moving along the cars towards them. That's why they were growing, coming nearer. He'd thought the wagons were hurtling towards the light, but the train was hardly moving at all now. How many lights? How many Cyclops-eyed creatures? He tried to count. Twelve, thirteen, fourteen. Fourteen blinding, staring eyes; fourteen hunched and moving figures.

No, he thought, no, that was insane, impossible. He was trying to shut out his thoughts, but all he could hear now was Dave Brookman's voice closing slowly over his mind:

He could raise the dead if he needed to . . .

And, Jesus, he could too. He could and he *had*. And he'd always said he was capable of anything. So now he knew what Stands could do; he knew it, and didn't want to know it. But, with the gloating lights almost upon them, it was Steve who asked the question he hadn't wanted to ask himself.

'How many? How many miners in that flooded-out shaft?'

Steve was holding a five-pound hammer aloft, but he didn't seem sure what to do with it. It wavered in his hand like rubber. 'But why? Why'd he have to go so far?'

'Because it's what you all wanted,' said a voice, behind them.

They wheeled around to look, hearts in mouths.

'You and the others in town,' said the voice, invisible, from the darkest part of the Dark Place. 'The

189

wives who wished them alive again. The dabbling old fools like Ruth who wanted to see life after life. That's what you all wanted, isn't it?' The dimmest, grimmest chuckle and then, 'You wanted your mine to be rich again, so look! I made it rich! You wanted your dead to walk again, and look! I got them walking!'

The shadow-man's high whooping laugh filled the tunnel.

The lights of the walking miners drew nearer, huddling around.

Then, without speaking, they were stumbling free of the paddy-car and down to the rasp and squelch of the roadway floor, Jules with his hand growing numb in Rachel's, Steve with his clanking rucksack, the hammer at his side. They stood there with nowhere to turn, walled in by laughter, walled in by dead, breathing miners.

'My sister, you stinking parasite!' Jules cried, and his voice almost broke to a higher pitch.

'Give her back, you've got no claim on her!' Steve Harper shouted. 'Give her back now! Keep those dead things away! Make things the way they were before!'

Rachel was silent.

Jules listened, frozen, hearing their screams and complaints resound through the tunnel like frightened creatures trying to escape. The Cyclops-eyed things had stopped or slowed behind them, and now he could hear their dust-wheezing breath, breath that scraped out as if it had claws. At least the laughter had died. Shouldn't he feel relieved by that? But then, as he looked, a new light glowed along the roadway where the voice must have been. It began very softly to spread outwards from a central point, just as it had in the fortune-tent. Suddenly he could pick out details in the glow – a hand, a crease in black leather, a blur of pale colour. It wasn't the light of a headlamp, or the rising glow of an oil lamp; it was light that seemed, oddly, to come from Stands himself.

In the darkness, a whimper, a scuttling of claws.

Jules felt himself grow weaker, unable to move. If Rachel squeezed any harder his hand would surely disintegrate. He gave her a nudge, tried to make her respond, but fear had paralysed her; she couldn't move either. Her dreams ended here, that was why. She shouldn't have come, he'd known that all along, but it was as if she'd known something he didn't, or had dreamed the worst and not told him. But why keep it to herself?

'Rachel?' he said, and the glowing light steadied and spread.

A small voice whimpered, 'Help me.'

Jules turned and looked sharply in front of him. Steve was readying the hammer high above his shoulder, waiting, not breathing. The small voice wasn't Rachel's, it came from the light where the shadow-man stood. Then he could see the white bundled blur at Stands's feet, the place where the voice came from. The pale little shape was Laurie.

He called her name twice and again.

'Jules!' she called.

'Laurie!' he called.

Their eyes met across the distance, and hers were so helpless he wanted to scream. She cowered on her knees while Stands held her fast by the hair. She was crying. The thing she called Toby sniffed and scampered about her, whining.

Steve levelled the hammer. 'Let her come here!' he yelled, and his yell went ringing and singing off along walls, under beams, into infinity.

'What?' Stands said. 'And have my little Laurie desert me? You wouldn't want to desert me, would you Laurie?'

Sobbing, she tried to struggle free of his grip, and Stands yanked her back by the hair. 'Yes!' she was crying. 'Yes I do!' She struggled again. 'I want to be with *them*!' She searched for Jules. 'Let me go, let me go! Jules, I thought he was good but he isn't! He isn't! He's bad! He's bad! Really he is!' And she struggled and screamed as Stands yanked her hair. 'Jules . . .' she pleaded.

Steve threw the hammer.

It was only a momentary distraction, but enough. Suddenly the hammer was whirling straight for the shadow-man's face, and Laurie was sliding, squirming, bolting free of the fist which held her, then running barefoot back down the roadway. She was running to Jules, but at first he didn't see her. He was staring at Stands in disbelief.

Stands never so much as blinked. His eyes were black-burning coals, his mouth still smiled. The hammer had passed cleanly over his shoulder, missing his face, and now it was swerving around like a boomerang, swerving and racing back where it came from.

Before he could move, Steve Harper was down. The hammer struck him somewhere about the chest and a great blast of air went out of him in a long sighing *ooof*. His limbs went splaying in all directions at once, and he dropped to the ground in a groaning pile.

The shock seemed to wake Rachel up. Releasing Jules's hand, she scurried across to where Steve was gasping, dragging for breath. 'Steve?' she said timidly. 'Steve, are you –'

At first he hardly stirred, as he lay where he was, gasping. Then he managed, 'Why, that lousy stinking scum-ridden . . .' And went on, reeling out a long string of atrocious words, some more atrocious than others.

'He'll be fine in a minute,' Rachel told Jules.

'Help him if he needs help,' Jules said. Laurie was with him now, clinging on like a limpet, arms thrown around him, dustily sobbing against his belly.

'He made me do it,' she sniffed. 'He did, he made me. He told me I'd see the New World, with all kinds of great things in it, but I didn't; he's a liar, he's horrid, I hate him! He kept me in here with those dead men, Jules, really he did. He made them come out of the walls and out of the floor!' She opened her mouth to go on, but instead collapsed into more tears.

'Keep her,' Stands said. 'She's done all I needed her to do.'

'Why her?' Jules challenged him. 'Why's she so special you had to put her through all of this?'

'Because she called me,' Stands replied. 'Someone calls, and I come like a faithful dog. Didn't I tell you that? Didn't you know it was her?'

At first Jules was dumbstruck: his mind felt blocked by the news, unable to think. He was staring at Laurie, whose eyes were wide and confused and helpless.

'You?' he said.

Tearful, she shook her head. 'I don't know any-more.'

'*You* called him here?'

Somewhere nearby, a rustling movement, a dragging of limbs in the dark. Jules couldn't see what or where it was, though he was sure it was Steve getting up. Behind them, the walking-dead miners were motion-less, watching, raggedly breathing.

'Of course she's the one who called me,' Stands was saying. 'She's the one with the power, aren't you Laurie? We made a good team. Laurie's wish-power, my gifts. We made it happen together. We put East-field back on its feet together.'

'That's all we need,' Jules scorned, remembering Brookman's vision. 'A town of zombies. We don't want your lousy favours here.'

'You'd rather I let things go on the way they were going? Without me, this town would be dead on its feet. They'd close it down in a minute!'

'Rather that than this.'

'You reckon?'

'I reckon.'

The shadow-man grinned; his light was a greenish haze, like that of the luminous skeletons back on the Scarborough ghost-ride. 'You know what you're saying, of course,' he said, his voice a stirring of bones and a sighing of wind. 'You'd rather stand by and watch your town slide than see something done to save it.'

'Damn right I would,' Jules said, calmly as he could. 'You want to know why? Because it's already finished. Better a dead thing stayed dead than this.

Things were bad enough before, but *this* –' He glanced at the Cyclops-eyed creatures. '– it's just bloody abnormal!'

'Do you hear what he says, boys?' Stands cried suddenly. 'Do you hear him, Paddy Richardson? He says you're abnormal!' The walking-dead miners lurched forward, grumbling, lights flaring, fingers reaching. 'You hear what he's saying?' Stands grinned.

Laurie was wailing. The space between Stands and the miners was closing. Even Stands was advancing now, moving towards them in small measured steps. Jules glanced about for somewhere to run, but it wasn't the fear that trapped him now; there was no room to move. If only he could think; if only they'd stop for a minute and let him think. There was something he badly needed to remember, something that Ruth had told him. He knew it must be important, but it wasn't there; it wouldn't come, it floated beyond his reach. He could only think of the miners behind him, their feet slopping wetly in damp and dust; and Stands was grinning, victorious, his eyes dark and dead as a shark's.

Rachel screamed; slippery fingers dragged across her shoulder and she wrestled herself away, squirming, and launched herself at Jules. By the time she reached him her scream was still chasing itself through the endless tunnels. Behind her, Steve was half up and trying to force open the rucksack. But that was no good, Jules thought; there was nothing inside that could help them.

'Tell her –' Rachel was gasping. Breathless, she had to fight to get out the words. 'Tell her she has to turn against him, tell her what Ruth said, tell her –'

But of course! Suddenly he knew what he'd needed to remember; it was their one chance, the one hope they had. What was it Ruth had said at the spook-church and hadn't been able to finish? *Perhaps the same kind of faith that made him strong can also make him . . .*

'Tell her,' Rachel repeated. She was watching the shrinking distance between herself and Stands.

Steve had the rucksack half open now, and was rooting around inside it.

'Laurie,' Jules said, forcing his sister to look at him. 'I want you to listen carefully, I want you to –'

But Laurie was crying, 'I'm sorry, I'm sorry, I wished and he came and he made it come true, I wished and I thought he was good, I'm sorry, I'm sorry I made him come, I'm sorry –'

'Laurie,' he urged, holding her gently. But he couldn't say more, for somewhere nearby, Steve was yelping and pulling away from the rucksack. He looked just in time to see Steve wrench his hand free and stand up sharply. At his feet the rucksack had fallen open; a mound of glistening black eels came sliding out.

Revolted, Jules had to turn away; but it was just another trick, just another piece of smart-arsed, show-off trickery. He had to ignore it and get through to Laurie. He cradled her in his arms, trying to help her understand.

'Laurie, I want you to listen, and I want you to do what I say. I want you to turn and look at Mr Stands.'

'I can't,' she shrieked. 'I can't, I hate him, I can't!'

'We want you to make a wish,' Rachel said.

'That's right,' Jules said, 'and this time it's a wish for yourself, not for him. Laurie,' he pleaded, 'if you hate Mr Stands so much, you'll turn around and look at him.'

But she buried her face deeper against him, sobbing.

'You can make Mr Stands go away if you want,' Rachel encouraged.

'Yes, you can,' Steve Harper put in, and perhaps Steve understood as well as anyone when he added, 'you can have anything you wish for, can't you?'

'Anything at all,' Jules agreed, and looked up. Stands had stopped moving towards them; and even the Cyclops-eyed creatures, whose grave-breath Jules could still hear and now almost feel on his neck, had stopped. Was there uncertainty among them? Did they somehow sense that Laurie could turn the tables? When he looked at the shadow-man, Jules could see anger in the face that had never shown anger, fear in the eyes that had never been fearful. Even the grin had slipped, and for an instant he thought he saw just a glimpse of the real living horror underneath. Briefly Stands's face seemed to twitch, though it wasn't a nervous twitch; it was more a shifting of flesh, as if all the muscles were scrambling to reshape themselves. The grin had slipped completely now; and now it was something else entirely, not a grin but a devil's grimace, the lips drawn back, white teeth bared like a dog's. At first it held Jules in trance, appalled and fascinated, but then he tore his gaze away.

'Listen,' Jules said, feeling the heat of Laurie's tears

and the tiny, tiny beat of her heart. 'You wanted him here, and now you don't –'

'I didn't know what he was,' she murmured.

'You wished him here, and now you can wish him away.'

'That's all you have to do,' whispered Rachel.

'That's all,' said Steve.

'That's all?'

'That's right,' said Jules.

'I can wish him not here and he won't be here?'

'That's right.'

A matter of feet away, the shadow-man's face was changing; muscles bubbled, eyes bulged like oysters. From the bared sneering teeth came the hissing of serpents, the snarling of dogs.

Lights were fading, walking-dead miners were backing slowly away. Could the dead be afraid? Could they really have anything worse to fear than death?'

'Jesus God we've got him,' Steve was shouting. 'We're on to him, we've got the creep, we have him where it hurts –'

'Hurry,' urged Rachel, reaching again for Jules's hand and grasping it tightly. 'Hurry,' she said.

'Laurie,' he said; and his sister was gradually raising her head, trying to meet his eyes. 'I want you to do this one thing, and that's all.' He sucked in coal-dust air, trying to steady himself. 'I want you to turn and look at him, Laurie. Remember all the bad things he's done. Hate him, Laurie. Hate him with all you've got, and wish him away. That's what I want you to do,' he said, 'you've wished him here, now wish him away!'

As Laurie turned, cries from the creatures went up

in the roadway, haunting the walls, beating against the stalled-out paddy-cars. They were helpless and strangely afraid, stumbling back in the dark with the lights on their helmets dimming, their cries becoming groans and sobs. Then Laurie was facing Stands, and somewhere between them the thing she called Toby was yapping and dashing about in a frenzy. She frowned; her meanest frown, the one she wore when she couldn't get her way, and pointed directly at Stands.

'You!' she cried. 'You! I don't like you anymore! I don't want you anymore!' And, making the wish, she closed her eyes.

The first thing Jules saw was the shadow-man's light fading. It seemed to burn inwards instead of out, retreating back where it came from. Somewhere among the network of tunnels, drips and creaks echoed, and a new sound gathered — a sound that Jules knew from before, from the day of the fête, the gathering war-cry of winds.

The shadow-man's face was barely a face at all now. The mask was gone; the thing seemed flipped inside-out, no eyes and no features, with only the mouth snarling back. For a moment the teeth parted, the mouth opened as if to speak, but no words came. Instead, out from the mouth rose a dark veil of smoke and the hissing of snakes and the baying of wolves; and the smoke was not smoke at all, but a black-beating storm of creatures with whistling shrieks, thrashing wings. They hammered blind against the walls and girders, fluttered hard against coal-filled wagons and dropped; some bashed into faces and hands and arms, or into each other, squealing, beating their wings. Then they vanished along the roadway, in panic and searching for greater and greater darkness.

Laurie was screaming, her eyes still closed, not daring to look. In front of her, Stands was beginning to sag like a beachball. It wasn't only his face now, but all the rest of him seemed to be caving into itself; he stood limp-limbed as a scarecrow, ready to drop in the gathering wind. Jules could only watch him, powerless. Surely the creep had no more tricks up his sleeve. Perhaps they should go now, right this instant, but he couldn't look away from the mess on the ground, not yet, not even to look at Rachel.

He knew she was there all the same. The grip of her hand was as firm as ever. She seemed to squeeze harder as Stands grew smaller and the winds in the roadway blew nearer.

Moments later, the rising force of the wind came charging towards them, through them, past them; it came with a whimper at first, and then a groan, then a scream. Jules closed his eyes against the hail of dust it brought with it. Winterish air swept his face, and ruffled his hair and clothing. And was that the voice of the shadow-man he heard, in the midst of all this, carried away on the edge of the wind?

I came from the last town, and after I'm finished I'll go to the next . . . I'll go to the next . . .

After what seemed an age, the wind was dropping, to a breeze, to a whisper, to nothing. He hardly dared breathe at first, even as it settled. Perhaps it was over. Perhaps, please God, thank you God, it was finally over.

The first thing he saw when he opened his eyes was that Stands had moved on. Vanished and gone. *Gone With the Wind*, he thought, and found himself, stupidly, wanting to laugh. Ah, *Gone With the Wind*, that was something Rachel had said when they kissed one night at the foot of the waste ground. She'd said it and laughed, and now he wanted to laugh, and did. The shadow-man was gone, wished away, blown as coal-dust to oblivion. Perhaps Rachel shared his amusement, for he could feel the firm squeeze of her hand, a reassuring squeeze. He wanted to hold her now, hold her and laugh and celebrate. *But save it*, he thought; *first we'd better get out*. For now he'd content himself with one brief glimpse of those deep chestnut eyes, remembering how he'd melted the first time she looked at him, remembering . . . how normal things used to be. So, with the light of headlamps fading, and the dust of walking-dead miners who walked no more mingling with the coal-dust they'd breathed all their lives, he turned to look into those eyes.

There were no eyes looking back.

There was no Rachel grasping his hand.

He felt the pressure of her fingers for a moment longer, and then even that was gone too.

Slowly, in disbelief, he sank to his knees, unable to stand. From far away, close but far away, he could hear Steve's voice as an echo of an echo: 'Oh Christ, Jules, I'm sorry, Jules, I never knew –'

But neither did I, he thought, as the tunnel faded to black once more, and the sighing of beams and the dripping of drops took over again with the storm now over, and Stands gone forever, and Rachel gone too.

Somewhere behind him Laurie, who couldn't be expected to understand, was scratching her head and wondering, 'Where's Toby? Where *is* he? Where's that girl you came with, Jules?'

'Jules, I never *imagined* . . .' Steve said.

He didn't hear anything else for a while, only the beat of his heart in his mouth, and his own scrambled thoughts. Who could've known, though? Who in their right mind would ever have suspected? He didn't want to believe it, but there the truth was – not staring him in the face, not anymore, but vanished and gone in the dust. So the out-of-town girl had come, like Stands, from out of the blue. And at last he could see what she meant when she'd told him, 'I don't think anything will come of it . . . I don't think I'll do you any good . . .'

She'd always seemed too good to be true, too perfect, too much the girl of his dreams. She hadn't broken sweat in the gym that day, and the fire on Moxon Street hadn't touched her. Maybe he should've suspected then, but he'd been out of his head too long. All she'd been was another trick, just another wish; something he'd secretly wanted and longed for; but after all that, she hadn't been real.

That was why her instincts had finally led her to Stands, why her dreams had been haunted by the Dark Place, and ended here. It was because, in a way, she belonged to Stands, she was almost a part of him. Perhaps, he thought, and this was the hardest thought of all, perhaps she hadn't even known what she was.

*

While the last of the headlamps faded, and darkness came down, Steve and Laurie were readying themselves to go. The cage couldn't be worked from down here; they still had to find a way out. Perhaps there were alarms to be sounded. If not, they'd have to walk the cold dark seams until they reached a connecting mine nearer Goldthorpe or Pontefract, and that would take hours. But that was the least of their problems. And now Steve was taking him by the arm, helping him to his feet and, further away in the darkness, Laurie was calling Toby's name.

'Shall we go?' Steve said.

─── *Epilogue* ───

Then there was Monday, a double French and Physics kind of day.

Jules sat alone at the kitchen table, his breakfast untouched, and craned his neck to see out of the window without having to stand. The sky was a cloudless blue, the Mount Temple houses a dullish brown, and on the ground the snow was beginning to thaw. In less than a day you'd see the town in its true charcoal colours again. The thought didn't exactly excite him, but it helped.

He was already fifteen minutes behind schooltime. By now they'd be conjugating French verbs that he'd never even heard of, but what the hell, let it rot, for a while. Eventually he'd go and catch up, but for now he was simply content to sit; he wasn't about to feel pushed. Today he wanted to loiter, take his time, remember how normal felt. Normal was something he'd missed; now he wanted as much of it as he could get, wanted to touch the old TV, touch the old Hoover, touch all the things that were just as they'd always been.

Upstairs, a creak, a groan, the click of a latch.

But that was Grandma, moving about. That was

normal. She'd been back since yesterday morning. She'd arrived two hours after the deputy from Goldthorpe had driven him and Steve and Laurie home in the NCB transit; and home they'd come, cold and coal-black and hungry, and after his parents had steadied themselves, setting aside their fears and their worries, the story had spun out all day and all night. 'Let's hope,' his father had finally said, 'that we're back to normal again.'

Normal was a good thing, sometimes a great thing. But it didn't and couldn't include Rachel, and that was a pisser.

Still, there were other things to look to, things that would help take his mind off her. Exams, for instance. And after exams the YTS, and after that ... Just who're you trying to fool, Jules Dwyer?

He sat for a little while longer and finished his coffee, which was cold. Outside, above the roof-tops, the sky was such a serene rich blue you'd almost believe it was summer. Then he realized it *was* summer; summer had been with them ever since spring.

At last he decided to make tracks. He was almost thirty minutes late now, but a nice easy dawdle down the waste ground would do. He doubted if Steve Harper would be in yet, anyway; they both had good excuses not to rush, though his mother had made a point of dropping Laurie at school before nine, and would probably drop her off every morning from now on. She would stay at the infants all day, if they'd let her.

He was half-way out of the door when he stopped,

noticing Laurie's walking-talking-peeing doll slumped in the wash basket on the floor, where she so often left it. The face was still pock-marked in felt-tip. Not knowing why, not really caring, he backtracked and picked up the doll, turning it around in his hands. *Laurie and her damn imagination*, he thought. *That's where this all started, isn't it? Laurie and her imagination.* He shook his head, half-smiled, pulled at the cord on the doll's back.

'I am Mandy,' the doll told him, 'and I'm feeling much better, thank you.'

That was normal enough too.

Leaving the doll in the kitchen, he went out through the door and closed it behind him, then walked down the path, past the sandpit, past the discarded toy dog on its wheels. A fine morning breeze blew into his face. It would warm through by lunchtime, and the thaw would accelerate. The snow in the gardens and gutters was turning, slowly, to slush.

At the bottom of the garden he opened the gate and stood for a moment, listening. Somewhere in the distance, a train was speeding towards or away from town. The fast train, by the sound of it, the one that never stopped here. He listened until it had passed and then, closing the gate behind him, he took off.

Well, *there* was gratitude for you!

One minute you were in, the next you were out; they wanted and then didn't want; they welcomed you with one hand while practically packing your bags with the other. You never could tell, could you, what some people really desired. Some didn't know their own minds at all.

Still, he'd shaken the dust of that glum charcoal town from his feet, he had no cause to look back. There were new and finer works to perform.

Stands sat in first-class, legs outstretched, feet lumped up on the balding seat opposite. His own seat was not reserved, nor did he hold a ticket, nor did it make a damn bit of difference. Now and then, a uniformed guard would roll between seats as he moved through the train, looking for tickets to check. Then he'd pass out of sight, looking for more.

There were five or six others in Stands's carriage – the usual pin-striped cigar smokers, some with important looking documents spread out on tables before them, one or two couched behind copies of the *Telegraph*. The guard stopped at each of them in turn, but he never so much as noticed Stands, for Stands didn't want him to. He merely walked on past as if blind.

Stands sat watching the country speed by – green sweeping stretches of country, basking in amber sunlight. But he'd soon put a stop to such niceness. Where next though? North towards Tyneside, northwest to the gently misted Cumbrian hills and lakes? Further north still, towards Scottish lochs and glens and the desolate folk of the islands; or south, to the cities, Birmingham, London, the English riviera of Bournemouth or Brighton? Somewhere, somewhere . . .

Wherever the caller was, that's where he'd go.

For somewhere a small distant voice, small but perfectly clear, called from the heart of the next town. He couldn't yet tell exactly where, but soon he'd know; soon he'd know a lot of things about the voice and its town, and all the people in the town. Soon it would be rushing along the track to meet him, and then he'd hear more clearly still. And then he'd know.

He sat and watched through the window for a time, and gradually his dark grin returned, as the first of the grey-looking storm clouds sailed up on the horizon.